Praise for *Crescendo*

"Crescendo *is a very special book. Written with the poetry and magic of an adult fairytale, this novel has all the elements that touch my heart: a love story that transcends lifetimes, the deep connection between animals and humans, reincarnation and the true nature of the soul, and the eternal value of kindness. Please give yourself the gift of this beautiful book.*"

— **Cheryl Richardson,** New York Times best-selling author of *Take Time for Your Life* and *The Unmistakable Touch of Grace*

"Crescendo *is a lyrical travel tale, a myth, a map, a parable—all of these and more. Amy Weiss has the skill of a poet, the dramatic flair of a storyteller, and the heart of a mystic. This little book is lit from within—lit with intelligence, spirit, hope, and mystery. Weiss weaves a spell that caught me in its luminous threads from the first word to the last. I feel expanded having gone on the journey of* Crescendo."

— **Elizabeth Lesser,** co-founder of Omega Institute and New York Times best-selling author of *Broken Open* and *Marrow: A Love Story*

"Amy Weiss's novel Crescendo *answers many real-life questions about eternal love, life and the afterlife, and our soul's journey in this wonderful once-upon-a-time story. A must read.*"

— **Char Margolis,** intuitive psychic medium and author of *Questions from Earth, Answers from Heaven*

"Deep, reaching and poetic, Crescendo *will invite you to reexamine your life, causing you to find new beauty and meaning in it. Weiss delves into the fundamental questions that are inherent to all our journeys: Why are we here? What is the meaning of life? Can what we love ever be truly lost to us? How are we connected? The answers, you'll find, are a gift that you'll take with you long after the pages of the novel are shut. Weiss is a powerful storyteller—and anyone who has ever loved or suffered loss will find comfort and meaning in her writing. Reminiscent of* The Alchemist, Crescendo *is a story of self-discovery and connection. The story Weiss writes is an important story for us all.*"

— **Laura Lynne Jackson,** New York Times best-selling author of *The Light Between Us*

crescendo

Hay House Titles of Related Interest

crescendo

A Novel

AMY WEISS

VISIONS

HAY HOUSE, INC.

Carlsbad, California • New York City
London • Sydney • Johannesburg
Vancouver • New Delhi

Published and distributed in the United States by: Hay House, Inc.: www.hayhouse.com
Published and distributed in Australia by: Hay House Australia Pty. Ltd.: www.hayhouse
.com.au • Published and distributed in the United Kingdom by: Hay House UK, Ltd.:
www.hayhouse.co.uk • Published and distributed in the Republic of South Africa by: Hay
House SA (Pty), Ltd.: www.hayhouse.co.za • Distributed in Canada by: Raincoast Books:
www.raincoast.com • Published in India by: Hay House Publishers India: www.hayhouse.co.in

Cover design: Neil Swaab
Interior design: Dave Bricker

An excerpt from "The Little Red Bird" in Japanese Nursery Rhymes by Danielle Wright
and Helen Arcman is used with permission by Tuttle Publishing.

Library of Congress Cataloging-in-Publication Data
Names: Weiss, Amy E., author.
Title: Crescendo / Amy Weiss.
Description: Carlsbad, California : Hay House, Inc., 2017.
Identifiers: LCCN 2016046664 | ISBN 9781401952969 (paperback)
Subjects: LCSH: Widows--Fiction. | Grief in women--Fiction. |
  Spirits--Fiction. | Immortality--Fiction. | Psychological fiction. |
  BISAC: FICTION / General. | FICTION / Visionary & Metaphysical. | FICTION
  / Literary. | GSAFD: Love stories.
Classification: LCC PS3623.E4548 C74 2017 | DDC 813/.6--dc23 LC record
available at https://lccn.loc.gov/2016046664

Tradepaper ISBN: 978-1-4019-5296-9

10 9 8 7 6 5 4 3 2
1st edition, May 2017

Printed in the United States of America

*"Death is only an experience through which
you are meant to learn a great lesson:
you cannot die."*
(Paramahansa Yogananda)

Once upon a time—

once outside a time—

two silvery souls stand on the banks of a mystical lake, deciding who to be.

The first one says, "How shall we love each other next? As brothers, lovers, neighbors? Let us be old friends or old flames. Or you could be a wolf, and I the moonlight who sends you into song."

"I'd like to be your husband once more," the second says, for it is here where marriages are made, proposed by the souls long before the bodies ever meet.

"Then I will be a woman, and I will be your wife," says the first. "Or I will be an oak tree. Or a little bird. Or the aria that it sings."

The husband soul laughs. "Why not be them all?"

"I will light a candle for you so that you can see through the darkness," the woman soul says.

"I will do the same," replies the husband.

"I could have a child," the woman suggests.

"You'd learn much that way."

"I could lose a child."

"That way, too."

A third soul hears this and swoops in. It wraps its wings adoringly around the one that will be its mother, never to leave her side.

A quicksilver soul dashes by, fluid and swift. It will be a horse, because its spirit wants to move. And it will cripple itself, because its spirit wants to move fast.

The four find themselves in perfect harmony.

The husband asks the woman, "How does this sound to you?"

She beholds her devoted spouse, the baby that will be born unto them, the mare that will spark them all into motion. "Like a beautiful quartet," she says, knowing that, at any time, any one of them can change the arrangement or compose something new.

The woman looks deep into the waters of the lake and listens to the melody of her body being formed. Her life will be filled with tension, for that is how the oak grows. Her life will be filled with lessons, for that is how the soul grows. Her life will be filled with love, for that is how we all grow. And her life, like all of our lives, will be filled with magic, for truly, what could be more magical than life?

In time, we will lose these memories, as the water will wash them away. If only there were something to remind us of the music we've come here to play . . .

LESSON I

}

Prelude

MAKING MUSIC IS AN ART. THIS BOOK WILL GUIDE YOU THROUGH THE PROCESS.

SIXTEEN BASIC CONCEPTS OF THEORY, TECHNIQUE, AND FORM WILL BE DEMONSTRATED, USING A VARIETY OF EXERCISES AND ORIGINAL COMPOSITIONS. MASTER ONE, AND YOU MAY PROCEED TO THE NEXT. OR YOU MAY CHOOSE TO STAY WHERE YOU ARE.

REVIEW EACH SECTION AND PRACTICE EACH PIECE AS OFTEN AS NECESSARY UNTIL PROFICIENT. SOME SKILLS CAN BE LEARNED IN MOMENTS; OTHERS MAY TAKE LONGER. PROCEED AT A COMFORTABLE PACE. THERE IS NO SET SCHEDULE FOR COMPLETION OF THIS COURSE.

TRANSPOSE THE PIECES AS NEEDED FOR YOUR PARTICULAR INSTRUMENT, AND DISREGARD ANY THAT SOUND DISSONANT.

LET US BEGIN.

The woman brushes the dust from the notation that waits to be played. The staffs are spidery, drawn by hand, as are the notes strewn across them. She hums these into a tentative existence, her fingers plucking the air. Although she will need her harp to turn them into music, already she can hear the richness of their sound.

The mare stands beside her, mulling a sugar cube in its mouth and regarding the woman with curiosity. The woman is curious too. What is this little textbook hidden in the hay? How many times had she knelt to tend to the animal's injured leg without noticing it? She asks these questions of the mare, who certainly would have witnessed someone reading inside its stall, yet its eyes give nothing away.

A melody makes its way toward her. It comes not from her book but from her husband. It seems made of light; then again, so does he, perched on a hay bale in the sun, strumming his guitar, spinning its strings into songs of gold.

She walks over to him and sits at his feet. His guitar rests on one knee, her head on the other. "Is this yours?" she asks, handing him the book. "I just found it in the stall."

He glances at the cover—*Music Lessons*, by Anonymous—opens the book, fingerpicks the piece that appears before him. "No, my little bird, never seen it before," he says, and neither has she, yet as she closes her eyes and listens to him play, there is the strange sense that perhaps this is not true. Then the tune twists into something gloomy and unfamiliar, the key changing to minor—as if such sorrow could ever be considered minor—and the feeling vanishes, along with the song. The husband has placed the book on the ground. His arms, once full of guitar, are now full only of her.

"That's much too sad," he says. "Sing me a love song instead."

As if every word she speaks is not a love song. As if there is not a love song in the way she looks at him, in his hands creating curls in her hair, in the touch of her cheek against his. A love song that has begun to form in her belly and that will, in due time, swell inside it. As if, each time he gazes at her, he is not sight-reading the music of her face. It is how they communicate, in that language of silence and sound. In the evenings they play together in the barn, where her harp tells of the quiet, naked things that hide within her heart, and his guitar shares secrets he did not know he had. They talk late into the night, their conversations becoming lullabies that send the mare, sleeping nearby, into dreams filled with desire and stallions and God.

The intensity of her husband's voice, of his eyes, of his child inside her is strong enough to push her soul slightly outside her body, where his is too, waiting for her. Love can be forceful that way, nearly too much for the body to bear, but what pleasure there is in its pressure.

"Sing me a love song," he says again, leaning down to nuzzle her, his head near that of his child's, and the woman has to laugh, because love songs are all that she knows.

. . .

She thinks she can hold no more joy, and then the husband places lilacs in her hands and a violet behind her ear. The wildflowers grow in the grasses alongside the house. For her wedding, she had braided their ancestors into her hair. On that day, they two had been pronounced as one: he was now she, she now he, a plural somehow also a single. An exhilarating riddle.

She enters the kitchen of the house, heading toward the sink for some water to quench the lilacs' thirst. He comes up behind her. Arms around her waist, breath against her neck. As she turns to kiss him there is a sudden surge, a spark flaring into full fire, and then nothing, nothing at all. Everything is black and still. The woman wonders if she has just died, cause of death an explosion of bliss, of kiss. But no, she is full of life; it is her house that is dead, the lights extinguished, the hum of electricity hushed. The heat of the summer is no longer willed into movement, and so it hangs, solid and stale, in the space between where the child's body begins and the husband's body ends.

With no lamps to keep it at bay, the night closes in on them. It takes over their home, their sight. It is everywhere.

And so is the husband. The woman cannot see in front of her face, but she can feel his. Her hands search the darkness and find him all around her. Proximity—it is love's promise, its power.

The violet falls from her ear. No one sees it happen except the child, who is watching from some equally dark dimension of its own, listening to the music made by the shadows as they sneak in through the windows and slink across the room.

. . .

The mare's whinny drifts across the unmoving air.

"Its leg," the woman says.

"Go," the husband tells her. "I'll meet you out there in a few minutes. I'm going to have a look at the fuse box first."

There is urgency, for she must tend to the mare, he to the house. Yet neither of them moves, choosing to remain, for one more moment, suspended in the silence. The woman lays her head on her husband's chest, hearing, without wanting to, his heartbeat. The sound is supposed to be a comfort, with its perfectly precise rhythm, its reassurance that all is alive. Isn't that what her child is said to be thinking of her own? But that would be mistaking a metronome for music. To the woman it is not solace; it is a slow, steady ticking toward death, an inescapable reminder that everything wound up must one day wind down. She places her hands on her belly to offset the thought, to assure herself that her family is beginning, not coming to an end.

Turning from him, she reaches for the counter and then the drawer beneath it, feeling for the candles and matches kept inside. Although difficult to do in her blindness, she finally manages to find flame. Her husband's features materialize. How ethereal, how beautiful he looks, wreathed in fire. It takes her aback: that small, soft glow in his eyes, in her chest.

With a last kiss he heads to the attic, the candle illuminating his path. She stays behind, lighting the rest of the tapers and placing them around the room. She takes none for herself. She can follow the fireflies, the stars, the beacon of the mare's cry.

And there it is again, more distressed than before. The noise quickens her steps through the kitchen, and as she hurries toward the barn the double door slams behind her. In the corner of her eye, she sees a flash of light. She tells herself that it is nothing, that it is a firefly.

It is not a firefly. It is fire flying.

Shorted wires. An overloaded circuit, a faulty switch. She will later come to hold any of them, all of them, responsible. The fault does not lie in them, though. It lies in her.

The force of the slamming door is not as strong as the force of love. It cannot push the soul from its body. It can, however, push a candle on its side. The flame takes a bite of the table-cloth, finds it delicious, and devours the rest. Its appetite is stupid, indiscriminate. The table, the curtains, the house, the husband: all go in its mouth.

The woman is unaware of this, for by the time the fire nibbles and licks the wires that the husband attempts to revive, she is inside the barn. By the time the house becomes newly alive, crackling with all the power that moments ago it had lacked, she is crouched down in the mare's stall. By the time her hand is on its leg, knitting its pieces back together, the legs of her house are splintering into shards. And then they can bear no more weight and, with a terrible crash that brings her running outside, they collapse. She does not know it—and then all too soon she knows it, and will never un-know it—but what she is hearing, along with the death of her house, is the death of her husband. The sound of him blazing, unfolding, transforming. She sees only the smoke, does not notice the sinuous plume of spirit that rises above it.

The fireflies and stars are there to guide his passage too.

In an instant she also exits her body. At least that is what she feels as she rushes toward the once-house, toward the once-husband, who is already wending his way up the summer sky. Surely if she were still inside it she would be able to feel her legs, which seem to have become as feeble as the mare's. Each time she tries to run they give out, and soon she can no longer move from the grasses at all. It occurs to her that this is what happens in her nightmares. A night, a mare—even words are coming undone.

That is all this is, she tells herself, *a nightmare.* It cannot be real. She will awaken at any moment, will discover that what she'd thought to be the blackout of her house was merely her descent into sleep. When the pain of a dream becomes too much, the eyes open, the blood floods with electricity and then relief. But there is no electricity, and the problem is not that her eyes won't open—it's that they are open, it's what they are seeing.

She leaves her body for a moment. The husband leaves his forever. They are not the only ones.

Baby bones are built to withstand the pressure of love, not the pain of life. For that, they need time to grow. A mother's misery deforms its little frame. A mother's tears nip at it with hopeless mouths. What more damaging birth defect could there be than sadness? The child must not be blamed; its house is gone, its father is gone, and most likely its mother is too. It extinguishes its life flame, no gentle wisp like that of the father but a red-hot rash on the grass, deeper and darker than fire and just as hot.

Is it the smoke that causes the woman to lose consciousness, or the shock, or the complete destruction of her world? Whatever the cause, she has no memory of what happens next. It seems to her that the grasses hold her in their arms for hundreds of years.

}

Dirge

*T*he woman opens her eyes to find dawn sober and subdued, as though the night were contrite for having set itself on fire. What an embarrassing display of gluttony! And with what consequence: the house gutted, the grass burned to brown. But grass feeds on fire. It has not been destroyed; it will grow again with renewed force. The same is true of the husband.

For a moment—a heaven of a moment—she does not recall what happened. Then she remembers, and the memory is relentless. Her husband is gone yet the farthest thing from gone, taking over every thought, leaving no room for anything but him. And how could he leave her mind when the smell of smoke won't leave her skin, when the very presence of her body reminds her of the lack of his?

It is one thing to lose love, and another to lose the possibility of it. In a matter of hours, all her selves have been ripped from her. She is no longer wife, no longer mother, no longer lover. What is left of her, then—simply soul? Though it is as if that too has escaped, has flown away to a place she cannot reach. That is what grief does. It steals the breath out of you, turns you as cold and lifeless as the one you mourn.

The earth beneath her is soaked with tears. *Very well,* she says to herself, *I will stay here and drown in them.* Despite her wish to cease existing, a being as small as an ant and buried deep within some remote yet vital part of her brain demands that she stand. The woman has never met this being before, this irritating creature that wants, above all, to survive. How can something so small and so far away overpower her? How can it even belong to her?

It may be little, but its strength belies its size. It forces her to her feet and makes her say good-bye to her child, who lies formless in the grass, never to be carried again. It makes her walk away.

There is only one place to go.

The mare, hearing the familiar creak of the barn door, starts pacing back and forth in its stall. It had kept its cries to itself all night long, aware of the trial by fire occurring outside, the metamorphosis of both the husband and his wife. The mare knows this in the way that all animals know such things. They do not blind themselves to second sight, the way people do.

When it sees her, though, a cry breaks loose. *I lost my family too,* it says without words, for horses speak not in words but in images. The ones that appear now begin gold and glorious and then fade to black. *I lost your husband,* they tell her, *and I lost the days when your children would ride upon my back into the orchards, and they would feed me apples, and I would feed them the wind.* The woman, however, is closed off to visions, and even more so to compassion.

An injured animal will often lash out in anger, an anger born from fright: the wounded dog bites the hand outstretched in help. And so two shaken animals stand facing each other in the barn. One inflicts the bruises, the other accepts them.

"Had it not been for you," says the woman, "I would have been inside the house. I'd have put out the fire, and my world would have gone on. My child would grow strong and my husband would grow old and my home would outlast us all. If I couldn't have done that, so be it. At least I'd have died along with them, and we'd still be together. You have cost me everything I love."

She feels fury. The fury is fear. Her blame is broad; it will settle on anyone in sight. It too is fear.

The mare hangs its head, offering the floor an apology. It does not need to look at the woman to see the cloud inside her, how it thickens with regret, how with each accusation she makes it wrests free from her body and enters its own. The mare allows it inside, because the mare loves her. It knows, in the way that all animals do, that anger is merely an attempt to discharge the cloud, and that both are equally insubstantial, and that both fog the sight. Besides, what she says is true. Hadn't its complaints inadvertently yet irrevocably separated her from her husband? *How could I have been so selfish*, it wonders, and the cloud encircles its leg.

"Let's go," the woman says, although she has no idea where. She simply can no longer be where she is.

The mare hesitates, on account of its disability and also its knowledge, which the woman does not yet share, that once they leave the barn they are never to return. Nonetheless, it follows her. It is willing to hobble itself, to exile itself, as penance.

First it stops at the spot where, a day ago, the woman had unwittingly begun her first lesson.

"No," she says. The music is lost. It has gone with the husband.

The mare stands firm.

"No," she says again, more a plea than a statement, but the mare knows what needs to happen and gives her no other option: they will stay stuck in place, or they will move forward. It is her choice.

Grudgingly, she approaches the harp. Its body is carved from wood. That is what fires are supposed to eat, a meal more fitting and filling than man. "Why couldn't it have been you that burned instead?" she asks, and as she does a fragment of her cloud affixes itself to the instrument, though to no lasting effect. The strings will transmute it. That is the alchemy of music: to take pain, that heavy, flightless stuff, and give it wings; to turn it into birds and release them to the skies.

She would have given up her harp forever in exchange for her husband, would have sacrificed one true love for the other, would have surrendered all its notes for a single note of his voice. Her hands are on its neck. She could strangle it. Instead, to her surprise, they caress it, as affectionate as ever. Love can be unconscious that way, automatic, even in the dark.

Then there is the book, lying on the ground where her husband had placed it. To think that he'd tried to close the pages on the sound of sorrow, and now it is all that she has left.

She picks it up and reads.

THE DIRGE IS A SONG OF MOURNING, A COMMEMORATION OF THE DEAD. IT DERIVES FROM THE WORD *DIRIGIRE*, MEANING "TO GUIDE."

LEARN THIS PIECE WELL, FOR IT IS THE FOUNDATION UPON WHICH ALL FUTURE LESSONS WILL BE BUILT.

PRACTICE IT NOW.

She slams the book shut. What nonsense! Death is mute; it speaks no wisdom, imparts no learning. To summon a song from its depths—that is magic, not music. She is tempted to return the book to the hay, to hide it for someone else, or from herself.

The antlike being has a better idea. It takes control of her hands, puts the book with the harp in the instrument's case, and puts the case upon her back.

At last, the mare moves. It is the woman's turn. She takes a final look at the life that she once led, then heads in the opposite direction.

•   •   •

He is not there.

Each day she opens her eyes to this blunt fact. Once it was he who woke her, and now it is his absence. Sleep is a force she crashes into, a violence, yet also a respite. In the mornings, grief is less raw, more tender; there is something about the sunlight that makes it ripen.

The mare and the woman walk alongside each other, while the months follow behind them. The woman feels as though she is crawling, for she lives just slightly above the ground. Grief possesses gravity, and sadness is an enormous hand pressing down on her. It forces her into two dimensions, flattens her breaths into sighs. The hand has no mercy. Once it finds you, it pursues you for life.

The grasses of the countryside lengthen into the trees of the forest. Yellow wheat turns to moss of an obscene green. The sun becomes tangled in the canopy of giant oaks and elms, whose branches shred it into slivers. Dusk steals in and colors the space left behind.

The woman makes beds of silver-maple leaves on which she sleeps, her pillow the mare's soft belly. The mare forages the ground for fallen berries though the woman eats little, for the loss in her leaves no room for hunger. It is its own fuel. It takes away the taste for food and gorges upon itself.

The mare winces from the pain of moving, the woman from the pain of existing. She begs the cardinals and starlings to silence their song; she cannot bear their stubborn hope. But the birds sing on, for birdsong is both impervious to pain and its antidote.

Autumn lights the forest on fire, and winter snuffs it out. The woman welcomes the frozen season. She understands what it is like to be ice.

She stops and lies motionless on the forest floor under the trees as the snow and weeks accumulate at her feet. Some days she can only look out from behind empty eyes, and nothing more. Some days the stupor wears off and she becomes the opposite, something far too alive. She is either freezing or bleeding, ice or fire, and neither is conducive to survival.

Some days she wonders if the end has come. This is not a fear. It is a desire.

. . .

To be alone is to lose language, for there is no one left to whom she can speak her thoughts. Thoughts grow wild in the mind with no one to hear them; they grow thorns. The woman listens to the rustle of the leaves, but they are talking to the wind, not to her. Words unheard will eventually dry up and stop making sound. If only her memories would do the same.

To be alone is to be a butterfly with a hole in its wing, every passing breeze a reminder that the beautiful part of you, the part that lets you fly, is missing. It is to lay bare the brokenness inside you, that wound which once was wing.

To be alone is to be a bottom-feeder, to dwell fathoms below the sea, where even the sun cannot reach. Where all that exists is wreckage; where all that surrounds you are old bones and other sunken sadnesses.

To be alone is to be dead while alive.

. . .

Spring arrives as an insult. The entire forest turns fertile. Life oozes in the mud, it squawks and grunts and croaks, it multiplies wantonly. The woman cannot escape this mockery of mothers and brides. Everywhere she looks, she sees fullness: the streams swollen with rainfall, the moon with stolen light. But she is full of nothing.

Even the worm in the dirt, which barely inches through existence, can give birth and give love. Who allows this of worm yet forbids it of woman? How can this lowly creature perpetuate itself again and again, and she not once? The worm has five hearts, so even if it were to lose a child it would survive. The woman had none to spare.

She wonders at this profusion of nature, at God's unfathomable humor—to exalt bees as queens and caterpillars as monarchs, yet reduce humans to ashes, babies to blood. To design such a world. To force us to live in it.

She can glimpse, inside the animals, the thrill of creation, which had lived in her too and then gone up in smoke. She can do this because she herself has been reduced to animal, to instinct, and her sole instinct is to panic, to climb the tallest tree and hide from it all. At the same time, to be animal is to be animate, to possess that most primal form of life, and she is sure that whatever is inside her where her soul used to be, it cannot properly be called life.

Spring becomes summer, the worm becomes grandmother. The woman and the mare trudge on, for how long she cannot say. Suffering turns time elastic, turns hours into centuries, turns every night into that one night, to be relived over and over.

One day, the sun disappears. She takes no notice of its absence; her world has long been missing warmth. The mare looks up and stops short, causing the woman, for once, to lift her eyes from the ground. In front of them is an enormous cave, blotting out all sky and all further progress through the woods. Its mouth is smeared with spider webs. She decides to enter anyway. The cave may be dim and stagnant, but so is life outside it. And she is tired of moving without actually going anywhere, of wandering the desolate landscape of loss.

Not so fast! A hound hurls itself out of the cave. Its eyes are bloodshot, for it knows no rest, only vigilance. A snake hides in its matted fur. The woman gestures for the mare to move behind her, though the mare needs no such instruction.

The hound lunges for them. Its jaws widen. The mare screams. The woman thinks, *All right, so it's death by dog.* But here comes that infernal antlike being again, reaching for the harp, unsheathing it from its case, plucking a string.

The woman is stunned. More frightening to her than the prospect of mauling is the prospect of music. She has not touched the instrument since her husband died. Can she remember how to play after all this time? Can one even play without a soul, and what kind of sound would that make?

She does not wish to try it now—or ever. But the noise has stopped the hound from biting, and the impulse to stay intact supersedes the impulse to stay silent. Like the hound, music has teeth, needles that sink under the skin. Unlike the hound, its needles sew as well as slice. They break you open not to hurt you but to heal you.

First she strikes a flurry of notes, any notes. The hound retreats. A tune emerges. It is rusty, for she has not spoken music in a while, and the voices of the woman and the harp are hoarse from neglect. Even so, there is no forgetting her first language, one that is more basic than words, and more truthful besides.

She plays by heart, letting its broken chords bleed into the forest and into the song. The antlike being conducts a mighty, manic concert, declaring with each measure the exact opposite of what the woman feels: *I want to live.* Her hands move without consulting her mind, flying from one note to the next. They start to glow with white light. The strings on which they land are made of silk, but they are also made of light.

Without stopping, she leans against an oak, unaware that it is listening. Though the oak is a strong, stoic type, it is deeply moved by the woman and the gentleness with which she cradles the harp. It is mesmerized by the strange spell her hands cast over the wood: transforming a tree into melody, making it sing. It yearns to feel her fingers brush against its own body, to hear the sound she would coax from its silence. Leaves fall from its branches, flutter around her, surround her in a sea of longing. The cardinals and starlings perched in its hollows cock their heads and stare. They have never known the oak to cry; who has seen their house shed tears? Their songs are also made of light—a different one, a gilded one, which erupts from their little bird bodies when they can no longer contain its force—yet they are unfamiliar with sorrow. Only the mourning dove knows its dreary refrain.

The rocks beneath the tree are listening. The sound hovers around them until they submit to softening. Piece by piece, their boundaries melt away, and soon they are rock no more but the merest memory of something solid. The disintegration is not distressing; it is relief. The woman would do well to follow their example. Despair is making her hard, it is making her dark, it is making her smolder instead of shine. Fire and pressure are supposed to turn coal into a diamond, not a diamond into coal.

The mare is listening. It has heard the woman play only songs of love, not of loss. Indeed, it is just beginning to learn of loss. Images flicker before its eyes in hazy shades of sepia: the wisp of a man spiraling into the sky; the touch of a mother's muzzle on its legs, urging them forward. *My mother?* The mare hungers for something that it had not even remembered and wonders where it has gone.

The hound is listening, sort of. It bypasses the sentiment in the woman's song and goes right for the pain. It knows pain. It feeds off it. The performance puts it to sleep, where it dreams of blood and death and other red things.

The snake coiled in the hound's fur is listening. The sorrow of the woman, the sweetness of the strings, the harmony that arises as the two twine together: they form an ache so strong that it pushes the snake out of its skin. In this way, art is like love, or perhaps art is love. The snake has not died, of course. It has merely shed its body in order to grow, just as the husband has done.

Is the woman listening? The harp's body runs down the length of hers, its shoulder pressed against her own. The soundboard sits at the precise place that once held her child. This is no coincidence. The music enters that abandoned house, reconstructs it, makes it livable again. It moves into the deepest part of her, beyond her bones and into her soul. Yes, her soul is still there. The hopeless times are not when it takes flight. They are when it takes root.

DIRGE. She did not need the book to teach her this after all, nor could she refuse to learn it. The bereaved know it intimately, instinctively. It becomes their entire repertoire; they are virtuosos against their will.

Her music comes to a rest. So, for a moment, does her misery. The audience members quietly reassemble themselves, tending to the sites where the song has slit them open. Even the hound sprawls on its back and presents its belly for a rub. This time the woman needs no prompting to take the harp with her. She places her hand on the mare's withers to guide it, and they both step over the harmless pup. The webs, weakened by the spiders' tears, fall apart at her fingertips, and she and the mare enter the cave. Together they navigate its unlit passages, feeling their way along the walls, oblivious to what lies before them. From the murk comes a voice that cuts through the cold air

"Here you are. Do come inside."

{

Lament

The two figures that sit before them say no more. Their massive bodies are carved from the cave and the darkness, shadow and stone. They are made entirely of rock: the spines that hold them erect are a column of boulders, the planes of their faces steep cliffs. Strands of black widows clasp their throats, a living, lethal necklace.

The mare staggers backward into the unfriendly embrace of stalactites, which dig their bony fingers into its flanks. Its eyes plead with the woman to retreat into the forest, but the entrance to the cave has sealed off, and nothing can pass through it: not light, not life. It turns out that it is not so difficult after all to stumble into the underworld. All one needs to do is follow the breadcrumbs that despair leaves behind.

Are we dead? the woman mouths to the mare. A flicker of hope kindles within her chest. The antlike being stomps its feet in frustration and puts it out.

"Are they here?" she asks. No one responds. But where else would her husband and child be?

She creeps closer to the two enormous monoliths, the king and queen of stone, and kisses the slopes of their toes. This is everything for which she has wished. "Please, are they here?" she cries, throwing herself at the queen's mountainous feet in desperation, in gratitude. "Let me see them. Return them to me. Let us all leave here together."

They are cold, unrelenting. Erosion is accomplished by years, not tears. What could be more stubborn and unyielding, what could be harder and more impenetrable, than stone? Only death. The woman is not being given what she wants, because death does not do that—it takes it. And now that there is neither air nor exit, it is going to take her too.

"I'm so sorry," she says to the mare. "I didn't mean to bring you with me."

The mare replies, *I would follow you anywhere,* for although horses speak in images, they are also fluent in love. What remains unsaid in any language is the haunting knowledge that its breaths are borrowed.

What does one do while waiting to die? The question applies to us all, though perhaps less acutely. The woman presses on the mare's back, urging it to lie down, to relax. She sits next to it and traces the contours of its aching leg, its tendons and its muscles, feeling them one last time. In her touch are countless apologies. They belong to the mare, of course, yet also to herself, to a life that had shrunk and atrophied to the point where it was no longer viable. How had she lost such control of it? She imagines herself as a newborn baby, for whom the future was supposed to be an open road stretching into the horizon, not a cave of remorse. *I'm sorry*, she says to her also. *You deserved so much more.*

The air thins. The mare slips into sleep and dreams of its mother. The antlike being is numb. It is petrified. It can't accept what is coming, but knows it's coming regardless.

The woman chooses to fill her last moments with song. Music and silence are intimately connected, complements rather than opposites. Silence is the predecessor; it mates with sound and gives birth to music. This time is different. First she will play the music. Then the silence will follow.

She takes out her harp and her book, the one her husband had once held in his hands. It is like touching him again. Soon enough, she will be.

Lullaby, Crescendo, Coda—some of the pieces are too complicated, too odd. She does not have the skill to play them yet, and now she supposes she never will. She pages through the earlier sections and comes to a stop on Lament.

A lament is a song for the dying.

There is no other instruction. She does not need it. Everyone she has ever loved is dying. Surely she has the skill to play this.

How strange it is, to perform one's own funeral song, or maybe it's less strange than sad. In any case, what choice does she have? No one is left to do it for her.

She smooths the page and begins. There is little light with which to read, though with her fingers sparking against the strings, with the faint glow floating from the mare's motionless body as it begins to die, there is enough. Songs of unconsciousness do not use much light. They could not stay unconscious if they did.

She does not even know what she is asking until the song asks it for her. *If I cannot have time with them, then let my own time end. If I cannot leave here with them, I cannot leave at all. You took them both. How could you forget me?*

Her hands sweep across the harp and become the white light, which wings its way to the king and queen. Sorrow takes flight from the strings, a mourning dove. The dove flies between the bars and perches on the notes, teaching the woman its tune. It has never mourned itself before, though that is simply a variation on the melody, a riff. Minor chords are the sound of crows being born. Harmony is the sound of one flying above another. They circle the king and queen and nest in the crags of their bodies.

The music reaches out to the queen and gently places a heart in the cavern of her chest. Then, with featherlight hands, it lifts the heart back out. Over and over the heart is removed, the heart is restored. This is what songs of sadness do.

The queen marvels at the sensation. She knows what the woman does not: that death is as dull as rock, no more intelligent nor worthy of grief. Yet the woman knows what the queen, sequestered in her cave for all eternity, does not: that death happens not to the ones who have gone, but to the ones who remain.

The queen's new heart grows a hairline crack. The lament seeps inside and widens it. She had always pitied these fleeting humans, doomed to live for hours instead of epochs, to tell time in biology instead of geology. Now one of them stands before her, praying for time to expire. The true misfortune, she begins to understand, is not to be born mortal; it is to love someone born mortal. She considers the flinty expanse of the king as she wonders what loss might mean. Mountains, after all, are seldom mourned.

Though his face is as blank as slate, something inside him is shifting. A pebble tumbles down the precipice of his cheek and crashes below. The ground crumples. So does he. The impact breaks the earth open. For this reason, songs of sadness must be handled with care; they can trigger disturbances deep below the surface.

The quake shatters the sealed entrance to the cave. What had once seemed indestructible is now rubble. Air pours in. The mare swallows it, ravenous. The woman scrambles to her feet and grabs hold of the mare's mane. This is their final chance, for the opening could seal over again at any time. She is astounded by her actions. The antlike being must have woken up. Or perhaps she has.

They are a step away from the threshold of the cave when the queen speaks. An avalanche of rocks and dirt erupt from her dusty mouth. What she says makes the woman turn around, leave behind all thoughts of leaving. What she says sends a tremor through her. What she says is: "The child was a girl."

. . .

The queen clears the debris from her throat. "She was the size of a whisper."

"A girl." It makes the child real. It makes the lament real.

"You would not be able to see her, not with the kind of eyes you have."

"A girl," the woman repeats, lost in the discovery of her daughter.

The king, still recovering from his earthquake, adds, "Your husband did not need to come here so soon. You could have had many more years with him."

The tectonic plates of the woman's body slide, threaten to buckle. "What do you mean? He wasn't supposed to die?"

"Not yet."

"Then why did he?"

The queen plucks a spider from her neck. She holds it in the broad hills of her hand and brings it toward the woman. Widow to widow, the woman and spider regard one another. The spider, slowly at first, spins its web on the queen's outstretched hand. A corresponding web takes shape in the woman's mind. The spider weaves the first strands. The woman sees herself meeting her husband, falling in love. The web expands; they marry, build their home. The spider is frantic, weaving madly, almost flying across the queen, connecting each of the silky pieces in a final, deadly web, and equally rapidly in the woman's mind the pieces of her husband's last day come together.

She lights the candle. The mare calls. She slams the door. The candle tips. She disregards the flash of the flame and continues toward the barn. The web traps prey. The fire traps husband. The house burns. The husband burns. The web falls into place. The web falls apart. The web falls from the woman's eyes.

It was she who asked the question, and now it is she who answers it. She lowers her face in shame, understanding that she is not just a widow but a black widow, and tells the king and queen what they already know: "He died because of me."

. . .

The hand of sadness had followed the woman through the forest, never once letting up its pressure on her back. Now a second hand joins it, the hand of guilt, and the two interlace their terrible fingers. It is difficult, nearly impossible, to bear the weight of grief, but to add the weight of guilt? The human body is not designed for this. The bones will fracture, the brain will flee.

"No," she says. *No. This cannot have happened.*

"Yes," the king corrects her. "You caused the fire." His words are matter-of-fact, and it is their factuality that pains her most. Life should be moldable, malleable. It should allow her to smooth her fingerprints from its surface and start over. Life is not clay, though. It is as solid as rock, set in stone. "The burns were severe, yet it was the smoke that killed him. He could not breathe."

The woman empathizes. She, too, cannot breathe.

"It isn't true," she begs. "It can't be real. What have I done? Please, please—" But death just sits there and stares blankly ahead, stony and silent.

. . .

For every shock there is an aftershock. To survive both is asking too much.

So, what now? the woman says to the antlike being. *How do I live with this guilt? And why should I be allowed to?* The antlike being is unsure how to reply. This is a problem, for if it does not have the answer, then how could she?

She can find no solution. Perhaps she can find a loophole. She runs her mind over her memories, listening for the sour string, the one that, if fine-tuned, would restore her life to harmony.

She thinks back to the morning before the fire, this time envisioning that she and her husband are far from their house, somewhere else. Anywhere else. Death comes calling, but they aren't home to answer the door. The electricity falters or it doesn't; no one is there to see it happen. When they return the next day, it is to a house full of sunlight, and so he goes on living.

She thinks back to the night of the fire. Instead of ignoring the attraction between the candle and the tablecloth, she rushes to pull them apart, and so he goes on living.

She thinks back to the evening when they first met, to a glance she doesn't acknowledge, a smile she doesn't reciprocate. And so he goes on living.

She thinks back to an afternoon when she had been cleaning the mare's stall, and a barn cat ran in with a blue jay in its mouth. She'd cried out, for she loved to watch the birds hopping through the grass, and here was the cat tossing its soft body in the air as if it were a rag doll and not a sacred container of soul. No matter what the cat did to it—picked it up, threw it around, tore its breast apart—the jay stared ahead, stared at nothing. Its eyes were wide open, yet they were vacant. It was this combination that disturbed the woman, that made her unable to look away, when all she wanted to do was look away.

The eyes. The eyes kept staring at her. What were they asking?

Now she knows. They weren't asking anything of her. They were preparing her. They were showing her how the jay's death— one of the most, if not the most, defining moments of its life— had been circumscribed in the life of the barn cat before either of them had even come into existence. How it had been written into the story of a tomcat brushing past a tabby, in the urgent desire, in the sex, the release, the love. In the kitten that started gestating in the mother, in the destiny that started gestating in the kitten. The jay's death was decided in a stranger before its life was yet begun. And then on a day just like every other day before it and ultimately unlike any other day before it, its fate collided with the now-grown cat. *Don't condemn the cat,* the jay was telling her. *It is merely following orders.*

This is what she'd tell the jay: The cat could have walked away. Destiny is the meeting, not the murder. And it, unlike life, is made of clay.

Before she met her husband, before they had even been born, she was already circling him like a cat. They were drawn to each other—not, as they had thought, to begin a life together, but to end one. Probability is not the same as inevitability, however. There were innumerable days, minutes, moments when she too could have chosen to walk away. If only she could spread them around her like a sea, turn back their tide. Then he would still be alive.

If only she could touch time, reinvent it, reverse it.

If only she had never loved him, then she could have saved him.

If only. If only. If only.

This is the most familiar song in mankind. Everyone knows it by heart.

• • •

The king and queen are watching a mind crumble to dust. It is inconceivable to them that a creature should be so fragile and soft. Then again, what do they know? They have never had to venture outside the cave or into the crevasses of the psyche. They are not the ones who must struggle like Sisyphus under the weight of accumulating indignities and atrocities. They have not felt the countless ways in which life is heavier than any boulder, a burden greater than stone.

The two of them reposition themselves on their thrones and turn to each other. The process takes ages, though at last they find themselves face-to-face. Something must be done. They cannot go on witnessing the unraveling of a soul.

The king speaks for them both. "Your husband has died. We cannot return him to life, but we can return him to you," he says, "if you will leave here and leave us alone."

The woman looks at him in disbelief. Could it be that death is less solid than she had imagined?

"I will," she says.

"He will trail your every step and follow wherever you go. He will be with you always."

The relief is physical. It becomes her breath, her bones.

"There is a condition," he tells her.

Her heart is in her throat, in place of her lament. "Yes?"

"You cannot look back at him."

"For how long?"

"The rest of your life."

"Then how will I see him? Or hold him? And how will I know he's there?"

No one responds. Death poses such questions; it does not answer them.

She hesitates. To what, exactly, is she agreeing? To never again see his face, to never feel the body she loved so much that one day, when she touched it, an entirely new body took form?

Yet there is no alternative.

"Give him to me," she says, and runs with the mare out of the cave before any of them can change their minds.

LESSON 4

~

Time Signature

Where is the husband? He must be behind her, though his footsteps on the fallen leaves make no sound. Is he back in his burned body or born in another: a gold-eyed fox, a moon half full, a melody come to mind? Would these be any less him— or more than before? Or is he a spirit, intangible and bodiless, a mist and a mystery? His return was promised. His form was not.

He is with her. This is what she has been told. That he is gone from her line of vision, not her life. Could it be that death does not have the power to separate, only to obscure—that love can be invisible yet indivisible? Then grief, too, would vanish from sight.

Still, he cannot be seen, touched, heard—only presumed. A person without a body is a belief. How can she know that he is there, that he is real? Can she love someone whom she cannot sense, or is that merely to love his memory? Like him, faith and trust follow somewhere far behind her, somewhere inaccessible. Doubt stays fixed by her side, a talkative companion that monopolizes the conversation, filling the lulls with its incessant questions, as though scared of what the silence might say.

Sometimes she wonders if he is there and a subtle breeze slides across her shoulders, the way his hands used to, or the trees that she brushes past smell inexplicably of coriander and clove, the way his skin used to. At other times she wonders what the space between them is like. How dense, how impenetrable the distance: if it is as close as a hair's breadth or as vast as a dimension. She wants to ask him what he has seen, but she is afraid he would answer her with blue-jay eyes or, worse, eyes of fire. That she cannot look back at him is, in some moments, a small mercy.

She and the mare and possibly the husband walk for months, though the forest around them stays obstinately the same. The maples remain maples. If they would just turn to palms! Then the woman would know that they were moving toward something, that they were moving at all. It feels as though they have been circling the same trees a hundred times, and that this is all the rest of her life will be: a continuous circle of loss and being lost. Perhaps it is not her husband following her wherever she goes but something even vaguer, like disorientation. How utterly absurd, to have lamented a life nearly cut short and then find that it is instead far too long, a never-ending walk to nowhere.

The mare favors its good leg and limps alongside her. It is dreaming with its eyes open, dreaming of limbs that fly. The woman watches its pain grow and feels helpless to keep it from spreading. She decides that there is no other option. They must stop this senseless wandering. They will turn around and head to where the house once stood. It may be a graveyard, but she is little more than a ghost. Even the cave would be preferable. She could collapse at the feet of the king and queen and ask them to take away her air forever. Then a reunion with her husband would be a guarantee, not a fantasy. Without legs, without bodies: it is the only way that she and the mare can run free.

For once she moves with direction, with determination, and as she does the landscape begins to change. The maples thin and become sparser. A glade peeks through them. Purpose is like a saw, sharp and precise. It cuts through the forest of the mind and allows a clearing to emerge.

The trees give way to wildflowers, the enduring to the ephemeral. A lake comes into view. Daisies and forget-me-nots decorate its border, while the sun sits above and threads diamonds across its fabric. At its center, an old man in red and gold robes floats on his back.

"Here you are. Be right with you," he calls out to the woman before descending below the surface of the water. Although he is far away, by the time his words reach her he has caught up with them. He and his gorgeous robes are completely dry, though his face swims in wrinkles. In greeting he sweeps his hand over the mare's mane. The mare feels that he has turned it to liquid.

The woman is confused. Has he been expecting her? How can that even be? "I'm afraid we're a little lost," she confesses.

"Lost? To be lost is to exist in a time and place—or, rather, not to—and there are no such things. You can only ever be in one place: here. And here you are, exactly where you are supposed to be."

He speaks the same language as she, yet to her it sounds incomprehensibly foreign. "And where am I?"

"Right here."

"Fine. I'm here. And once I pass through here, then I'll be . . . ?"

The old man laughs, delighted. "Here, of course. Where else could you be?"

The forest may have been a labyrinth, but so is the old man's mind. It ensnares her more than tree branches ever could. "I've had enough of this," she says to him, and to the mare: "Let's go."

"How can you go anywhere when you are already there?"

After all that progress, this is what finally stops her steps. She has survived suffocation only to be felled by a riddle. She sits down where she is and rests her aching head in her hands.

The old man kneels, lowering himself to look in the woman's eyes. His own are as calm and deep as the lake behind him. He recognizes her disappointment. So many are disappointed upon finding themselves here, always wishing to be somewhere else.

His voice is patient, his kindness plain. "You are at the lake of time. It's a man-made lake, naturally, though don't let that deter you. It's a pleasure to experience. Come on in," he says, taking her hand and leading her toward it. "The water's fine."

Indeed it must be, for as she approaches she notices people swimming inside, pulling themselves onto its shores, resting on its banks.

She leans forward, cautiously dips a toe. The water is neither warm nor cool. The water is a memory. It arrives in waves, it laps at her awareness, it pulls her in and out, in and out.

> My mother sits at her vanity. I sit at her knee. She is dressing up for an evening out with my father, spraying perfume on her throat. I become drunk on its scent. She dusts powder on her face, then playfully sweeps the brush across my nose. I feel as though she's just sprinkled magic on me, the magic of being a grown-up. How I long to know this secret world myself, this world of dancing and starlight. Her laughter flutters around me like butterflies. She leans down and kisses my forehead, and the smell of her is intoxicating, it is bergamot, it is woman—

As suddenly as they have come the scene and the scent are gone, the woman not in her childhood home but in some strange lake, not with her mother but with some strange man, and she asks him, "What was that?" and he says, "That was time."

. . .

The old man wades into the lake, his voice and his red and gold robes trailing behind him. His head disappears below the surface, and when it reappears it is the head of a beautiful young woman dripping in gold and rubies. Once more he immerses himself, and now he is an infant, swaddled in red and gold cloth. With a last plunge he becomes the old man again, and as the wrinkles re-form on his face, so does his smile.

The mare watches with a thirst. It too approaches the banks and places its soft muzzle in the water.

> The world a white bubble, bursting in a field
> of sunflowers. Shaky legs. Healthy legs. Warm
> bees in my ears. My mother, singing to me
> with her eyes.

Startled, it raises its head, then drops it to drink in more.

"Now your harp," the old man tells the woman.

"But that's inanimate."

"Is it?"

She flinches at the thought of doing what he asks. To submerge a harp in water is to kill it. Its wood will bend, its tone will warp. She has already caused so much death. She cannot be responsible for more.

The old man nods his encouragement. This is not meant to stump her. "Isn't it time to move past dirges and laments?"

She has to admit that it is. Even silence would be better than another song of mourning. She shuts her eyes, holds her breath, and lowers the instrument into the lake.

Then she peeks.

The harp is no longer made of willow—it is the tree itself. The roots of its chords lengthen into the roots of a trunk. It weeps leaves instead of notes. It is said that a willow grows where the ghost goes, that its branches are used to sweep tombs, to summon the dead back to earth. Of course this tree became her harp. Nothing was more suited to sing her sorrow.

Thirty-four strings once looped themselves through the instrument. Now thirty-four mulberry moths cluster around the tree and lay eggs upon its leaves. A newly hatched caterpillar looks around and cries out with dismay. *I cannot find my wings.* It works itself into a frenzy, desperate to transform the body it was given into the one it was promised. *I'll lock myself in a fortress, lest anyone look upon me and think me worm.* The cocoon that it spins undergoes its own transformation, turning into silk, which turns into string, which turns into song.

The song, too, must come from somewhere. Before it arises in the instrument, it arises in the musician. The drone of her daily life, the plainchant of her midnight prayers. The G major of her quiet satisfaction. The flatted fifth of goose bumps rising on her flesh. The minor scale of her sigh, its origin sadness or sound, whichever comes first.

The old man signals for the woman to lift the harp from the lake, and instantly it resumes its shape: the willow shrunk in size, the moths a memory. Then he takes hold of *Music Lessons*. With a reflex she didn't know she had, she knocks it out of his hand. The harp may be undamaged, but her faith extends only so far and not beyond the book. So few things belong to her anymore. The fire has taken most of them away. She will not let the water take the rest.

He understands. If she would trust him to show her, then she'd have the answer to a question she's yet to even ask. But she'd rather have the riddle, and he's pleased to play along.

The woman stoops down to pick up the book, glancing at the page to which it has fallen open.

WATER, FIRE, EARTH, AIR: THESE ARE THE ELEMENTS OF CREATION. IN ORDER TO CREATE HARMONY, KEEP THEM IN BALANCE.

WADE INTO THE WATERS OF TIME. FIRE IS A SOURCE OF ENLIGHT-ENMENT. LET IT ILLUMINATE YOUR PATH. RETURN TO THE EARTH AGAIN AND AGAIN, EACH TIME WITH THE LIGHTNESS OF A MOTH IN THE AIR.

THIS IS HOW MUSIC IS MADE.

She looks up from the words. A little girl is knee-deep in the water. In one hand the girl holds a willow catkin; in the other, sugar cubes for the colt beside her to nibble. She hums an old, familiar tune. It travels on air scented with bergamot perfume toward the woman. The girl waves to her. Time ripples across the lake.

"What is this?" the woman asks. "Our childhoods?"

"There's much more in there than that," the old man says. "Go deeper. You'll see."

He motions to the shore, where a man stands ready to dive. They watch as he enters. He stays inside for a bit, climbs out, dries off, dives back in. The man does not change, but his dive does. First it is a belly flop, because he does not know what he is doing, or he is scared, or he simply wants to create a splash. He tries again, something more complicated; he uses different muscles, he perfects the technique. Then every dive becomes one of sublime beauty. Until then, though, what an awful mess! All that splashing around. All that fun.

Sometimes others join him for a synchronized swim.

Sometimes they thrash in the water, and he jumps in to bring them to safety.

Sometimes he just floats on his back for a while, relishing the warmth of the sun on his face.

The old man says, "That swimmer you have been watching, does he die when he gets out of the water?"

"Hardly. He rests, or he goes back in again."

"Do you grieve the completion of each dive?"

"Grieve it?" What a thought. "No, the dive begins and ends, but the swimmer does not."

"And would you drown yourself in guilt and sink like a stone," he says, "if one swimmer left the water while you remained inside?"

The woman turns to the old man. He is looking intently at her, waiting. He can wait forever. He has the time.

. . .

The lake is thick with movement. Its banks are dotted with silvery, birdlike things, things made of light. As they glide inside the water, their light becomes cloaked in bodies, and their wings of mercury grow heavy and human.

"These beings—they're all dead, then? And they go in the water to come alive?" the woman asks.

The old man shakes his head. "The soul is not dead, nor is it alive. The soul just *is*."

Her voice snags on sadness; a little piece breaks off. "What of my daughter? She was in the lake, she must have been. Did she surface too soon?"

"She was testing the waters, but it wasn't right."

"For her."

"For her and also for you. To leave: that was her gift to you."

A *gift?* To lose one's child?

"Now she reaches for you from outside the lake, rather than within," the old man tells her. "What's the difference?"

The difference is time. The woman could have spent years upon years with her child in her arms. Years in which her daughter was an actuality, not an abstraction. When she was not blood spilled on the grass but blood contained in a body, a healthy, vibrant body that grew and ate and skipped through the fields and let its hair grow long and dreamed thirty thousand dreams and wept and fell in love, or fell in love and wept. A body that belonged in time, not beyond it.

The old man knows that time is a figment, a fiction, a gossamer cloud blowing through the mind. What else could something so elusive and erratic be? The woman's years are made of months. Elsewhere they are made of light. Her years are different from those of the ancient nomad, who, by counting moons instead of suns, discovered that he could live for centuries. Man carved time into zones, placed an imaginary line in the ocean and called it a day. What an amusing puzzle! To the old man, time is no more than the blink of a dinosaur, the shake of a lamb's tail. But to the woman it is something far more concrete and cruel, a monster she both fears and craves; it destroys, yet there is never enough of it. Her child is not its sole victim. It steals all babies, puts adults in their stead. It tells them to leave their homes and their mothers. Then it takes away the mothers. It turns everyone it touches to an orphan, and it ravages the ones who are left, leaving its track marks all over their bodies.

The woman's eyes are watery like the lake, though less clear, muddled with something human. "I think I'd prefer to remain on the shore. I don't know why I ever would've gone inside at all."

"Because you wanted to listen to the concerto of a summer storm and hear its notes on your skin. And taste the exquisite pleasure of wild blackberries as their juice trickles down your arm. And see how a lady's slipper catches the dew and feel how a lover's smile catches the breath. Because only in a body can you make song, and move your body to the song, and revel in the dance. How else are you to experience all the staggering beauty in this world?"

"And all the death and the loss."

"And the love."

"And the grief and the pain."

"And the love."

She groans. She'd rather not exist; must there be such an argument about it? "My husband promised me forever, then vanished into a plume of smoke. If love is any reason to live, surely it should be stronger than fire, than flesh. Now I'm told that I cannot even look back at him. What kind of love is so slippery and shy?"

"In a sense it is true that you cannot look back, and in a sense it is not."

Another riddle?

"Go in the water," he instructs her. "Look back that way, much farther back."

"Into my past?"

"Into all the pasts you have ever had."

The woman regards him with astonishment, but the old man just laughs and claps her on the shoulder and says, "You think we get only one chance to dive? Now what would be the fun in that?"

≀

Da Capo al Coda

*M*y skin is like an onion, paper-thin, peel-ing away. After all, I have worn it for ninety years. My teeth left long ago. I don't mind how time strips such things from me, for look at all it has given: grandchildren upon grandchildren, an anthill of a family. My sons carry my face in theirs, though they are children no more. Now they have freckles for hair. A woman brings me my evening rice. It is my wife. She is as ancient as I. When my spirit leaves my body and becomes a cloud, it is she who, rather than feel the rain on her face, follows me up the sky.

"Look in her eyes," the old man says from above, his voice distorted from traveling through so much water, so much time.

> I try, but her smile makes them hard to see. *Open them*, I ask her. As she does, the recognition knocks the wind out of me, and I am forced to swim upward, to find air. They are the eyes of my husband. The eyes I am forbidden to turn around and see. The eyes I believed I would never see again.

The woman reaches the surface of the lake, breathless from the dive, from the discovery.

"Go deeper," the old man says.

> A rickety train takes me to my schoolhouse. It is morning, yet so early that it is still night. I am young, the train is old. The windows are glassless and put up no fight against the wind. I close my eyes to feel safe, but the train jerks and speeds and I cannot rest. Today will be my first day of school; I cannot rest for that reason either. At daybreak, I rise and walk down the aisles. Another schoolchild, a girl like me, wears the same blue uniform, her black hair in braids against her head. I want to ask if I can sit

with her, though shyness prevents me. Which is worse, to have to ask this of a stranger or to sit by myself, alone and cold? She doesn't need me to ask, anyhow. She simply smiles and pats the seat next to her, and I slide in with equally wordless gratitude. She takes a wool blanket from her satchel and spreads it over herself and also over me, tucking in the corners around my shoulders so that it stays in place. For the first time I look around and see the mountains sparkling like gold. The sun lights up the blanket. It lights me up too. My head turns heavy with fatigue and falls on the girl's shoulder. Through the fog of sleep I hear her singing a song: *Little bird, blue bird, why oh why so blue? Because it ate a blue fruit.*

We will be in different classes, for she is older than I and more advanced in her studies. Our rooms will be on opposite sides of the schoolhouse. Occasionally I will see her when we break for tea and mandarins. We share smiles, never words. She will finish school, and I will marry a local merchant. We will not meet again.

The old man's voice echoes across the lake. "Who is the friend?"

I go back in time, I go back on the train, I go back up the mountain. *Wake up,* I tell the young schoolgirl that I once was. *Open your eyes.*

I open my eyes. I look at my seatmate. My seatmate looks back at me.

My husband looks back at me.

I am a lotus. It takes a century for my toes to reach for the ground beneath me, a century for my hands to reach for the sun. A dragon-fly visits me one summer. We spend the long hours of the days together, locked in a quiet caress. They are the happiest months of my life. Through him I, anchored so tightly to the mud, come to know flight. I am his hammock and his refuge; his stained-glass wings are my church. He dies in my arms. I hold him for a thousand years.

The night is deep and silent except for the drumming of my heart, which rattles my body with its force. I am sure the moon can hear it. I look down at my bare feet. *Don't be so afraid,* I tell myself as I walk toward the elder's hut, but my feet do not move of their own accord.

A torch is lit. The darkness flees like a dream. The fire animates the faces of my tribe.

I wish someone would put it out, for at least in the dark I was blind to their disapproval. One of the members will not even look at me: my brother. We are all family here, though he alone is my blood.

That morning there had been a hunt. All the men took part. I snuck off, even though they needed me for my skill with the spear-thrower. My brother is also good, the second-best hunter in the land, although they never give the spear-thrower to him.

I went straight for the wild beast. No one had seen her except for me, for my eyes were gifted to me by the hawk. I crawled to her, told her to run or be slaughtered. I knew that she had just birthed calves, and that her death would mean theirs. I had watched the calves be born and reared and loved; they were as tender to me as my own. I hissed at her and made a giant of my body. She stared at me, uncomprehending, then lumbered off. The men were still on the hunt, and I slipped silently alongside them.

Someone had sighted me. I knew it in the way all prey knew it: in the terror that fizzes in the belly; in the fear of the unspeakable coming to pass, in the acceptance that it has.

I recognized it from my nightmares, where I'd seen the face of my death and learned its contours.

It was my brother. He would never give me away. I was safe.

I was wrong.

In the elder's hut, my body is cold with dread and hot with fire. Everyone blames me for the unsuccessful hunt and for their hunger, and rightfully so. I valued the life of the animal more than the life of my tribe. I betrayed them by denying them their sustenance. I betrayed them by being born a man too weak in the heart to hunt, worse than woman. "Vision of hawk, courage of mouse," they chant, though their song is joyless.

They do not kill me, but they do not let me stay. Where will I go? There is only open plain, and desert beyond that. I will be alone in the emptiest place on earth. Even the stars are disgusted and turn their backs on me. It is a death sentence by another name, a longer one.

I look around at the others. Their faces show no sadness. I walk toward the one that most resembles my own. The spears and the glory will be his now. I look into those December eyes, black and frozen.

The eyes of hatred.

The eyes of my husband.

We are being handfasted, he gives me a ribbon
and I give him my troth

and

I am the lowly monk, he wears the saffron
robes. I scale the cliffs to learn the secrets of
his breath

and

I bear him from my body. When I hear his
first wail it is like the stars are exploding inside
me, I had not even known I had stars inside me
until that moment

and

when he dies I believe he will come back to
me as a crow. I search the skies every day for
his return

and

he is my teacher and he is my neighbor and
he is my sister and he is my husband and he is
my wife and he is my child and he is

Once she'd left the cave behind, the woman had assumed
that she would do the same with her grief, that she would trade
its company for her husband's. "He will be with you always,"
the king and queen had told her, and she took their words for

truth. She spoke to him, she cried out for him, she reached out for him. He never answered. She sought him everywhere and found him nowhere. He was with her, but his presence was not. His humanity was not. The bounce in his gait and the timbre of his voice and the hollows carved from his collarbones were not. What did his return mean, if none of those things had returned along with him? Every response of his that she didn't hear, every glance of his that she didn't catch, reminded her of what was missing, of what had been lost—all those indefinable qualities that differentiate a man from a phantom. And so, unlike him, grief refused to let her walk alone. It slithered alongside her, tracking her with its unblinking reptilian eyes. It coiled itself around her legs, constricted her, squeezed the life from her.

DA CAPO AL CODA MEANS "FROM THE HEAD TO THE TAIL," LIKE A SNAKE. PLAY EACH PASSAGE DA CAPO AL CODA—FROM THE BEGINNING.

How often she had read these lines in her book, thinking them an instruction when they were a prescription. Go back to the beginning of your love song, and play it over and over. This will release the pressure. This will sheathe the fangs.

She had thought that she would never touch her husband again. Now she finds that she cannot touch a life without touching him. She has been so many people and feels she can hold no more inside her, though she has merely skimmed the surface of the water and of the self. Her body has stopped swimming. Her mind has not.

The old man sits peacefully on the shore of the lake, awaiting her return. The woman thinks that she has been in its depths for an eternity. For him no time has passed at all.

"My husband is everywhere," she begins to tell him.

"Yes," he says.

· · ·

The woman fingers the tangled threads of her pain, smooths out their knots. Her husband has died repeatedly—*the strands start to knit together*—and with each new birth he is returned to her, not as a favor but as a rule—*the pattern presents itself, the design takes shape*—and if there is no death by old age, and no death by exile, then what is death by fire—then what is death?

She sews and she spins. The threads arrange themselves and fall into place. The white light arises from her hands, which are already familiar with these motions, for a harp is a loom that weaves notes instead of cloth, that turns the material of misery into music.

And life, too, is a loom, the soul the shuttle, she the warp and he the weft. They cross each other, they clasp each other, they weave in and out and through each other to create a blanket that covers the shoulders and the stars. Over and over the weft passes, and the warp separates in two. One layer is raised, the other lowered. With enough repetition, a fabric is formed. Over and over the body passes, and the human separates in two. One layer is raised to the sky, the other lowered into the earth. With enough repetition, an angel is formed. The bereaver calls this dying; the weaver calls it shedding. She understands the rhythm, is aware that the separation is temporary: a pause of her breath, a flick of her wrist. She knows that the threads are not coming apart but preparing to come together. They are not fraying, they are not unraveling. They are stitching the tapestry of time.

. . .

She is the lotus, he the dragonfly, I the breeze that propels him into her arms.

I am a maple leaf, renouncing my branch in order to fly. This is the moment of my death, for I will no longer have roots on which to feed, yet every day has led to this leap and I am unafraid. I let go! The wind leads and I follow; it dips me and I twirl. I am dizzy with joy, enamored with sky. The dance must end, though until then—freedom unlike any I have ever known. The grass catches me in its arms. We dissolve into laughter and leaf. The sun melts me away and the earth feeds me to my brothers on the branches, those who watched me die, those who watched me fly.

I am a sailfish. I didn't know that anything without legs could run as powerfully as horse, yet without land to slow my steps I become a weapon, slicing the waters like steel. My body is a bullet, sleek and streamlined and gunmetal gray. I am gasoline on fire. I am fast enough to catch everything except the sun. I spend my days stalking it, jumping wildly in the air, never catching it, always trying.

The mare's soul is born to move, to hurl every possible body against the wind, to be the wind. And now it is lame, prevented from doing that which it loves the most. How better to truly learn the nuances of movement and of freedom?

The woman feels horrified, responsible. She has crippled the mare more than any injury could: forcing it to endure her journey, asking it to lay its freedom at her feet, reining in its birthright to run. It seems to her that it is she who is running blind and reckless through life, depriving the ones she loves of their bodies.

But the mare knows that every plodding step it takes alongside the woman pushes her a tiny bit farther, higher. An animal heart does not have the same boundaries or conditions as the human heart. It is more tolerant, more transparent. The human is to learn to remove the limits on her heart. The animal is to show her how. This too is a lesson in movement, and in freedom.

. . .

"The dragonfly was my soul mate, as was my ancient wife. Why would my husband come back to me as a schoolgirl on the train," the woman wonders, "as a classmate instead of a soul mate?"

"Who but a soul mate would drape you with kindness so that you could rest? Who else would agree to take on time with you—and for you?"

"Wouldn't a soul mate be forever? I never saw the schoolgirl—him—again."

The old man is puzzled. "Never saw him again?"

She recalls the failed hunt, the exile under the stars. Her voice and her eyes drop to the ground. "You mean to tell me that a soul mate would be so disloyal, so hateful."

"Who *but* a soul mate would lower himself for your learning? Who else would allow you to experiment with pain and with hatred, and do this for you out of the highest form of love? Don't forget: the same brother who betrayed you is the same wife who gave you companionship, the same schoolgirl who gave you comfort, the same husband who gave you music."

The serpent of guilt sidles up to the serpent of grief, touches tails, takes its place. "I can't blame him," she says. "I took away his body. I took away his child. Whatever he did to me in the past, I've done much worse to him in the present. I'm the one who must be punished, who must make it up to him."

"Oh yes, punished. Make it up to him. That's a good one! What was his punishment for betraying you? To cover you with blankets of sunlight, to lavish you with grandchild upon grandchild, to braid wildflowers into your hair and happiness into your song."

The old man waves his arm in front of her face. Scenes appear in its wake, transforming so fast that she can scarcely make each one out before it disintegrates. A home far out on the steppes, a man's hands, a sharp knife. A mother and child, disembowelment, blood on the dirt, on the knife, on the man's hands—her hands. She brings them to her lips. The blood tastes of iron but it is mixed with another taste, a more savory one: pleasure. It is too strong for her to stomach.

"You have forgiven yourself for these actions," the old man says, "but not for an accident of physics, of flame?"

The king and queen had convicted the woman of a crime, had brought her to her knees with remorse. Now the old man performs the same spell. "That man, that butcher—that was me?" she utters, the sound coming from some low, dim place inside her, someplace the antlike being cannot access. She suddenly wants to run from this lake of time, afraid of how many other murderers might emerge from its depths, clutching candles and knives, wearing her face. "And you show me this so that I judge myself *less?* I am unforgivable. I shouldn't be allowed to live, to keep coming back."

"No. You are learning. What you did then, others do now. They are also learning. And because there is no time, there is no difference between then and now, or between you and them. We've all given life and taken it. This hand thrusts a knife into an innocent belly," he says, tapping her left hand, and then her right, "and this one extends alms to the hungry. The same person who slays a mother and her child gives its own life to save a beast and her young. Marvelous, isn't it?"

The woman does not find it very marvelous at all.

The old man leads her back into the lake, guiding her shoulders beneath its surface. In its waters a reflection appears, a mirror of time. She sees herself as a young girl, dressed in a white pinafore and sitting cross-legged on the floor of her kindergarten class.

"You knew so little then, in a way," he remarks, watching the girl with paternal fondness. "You could not read the literary classics or the periodic table. You were just starting to learn how to share with others, to wait your turn, to care for your body and figure out what it's capable of doing. Was that unforgivable?"

"I don't understand the question."

A boy in the classroom hunches over a toy guitar, pulling its strings until they squeal. The little girl, intrigued by the sound, bounds over to him. She wants his toy. He stands in her way. When she asks to have it, he declines. So she shoves him and he falls to the floor, crying in displeasure. He considers kicking her or throwing a temper tantrum, although he decides against it.

"Were you unforgivable?"

"I was just a child! I didn't know any better."

A teacher walks up to the children. She pats the boy's head and lifts him to his feet, then turns to the girl.

"The teacher ought to kill you," the old man suggests, and the woman gasps. "Isn't that what you said? Or she could put you in a time-out for all eternity, though there's really no need. Even the most disruptive student will sooner or later get her act together and move on to the next grade." He stops speaking as the teacher kneels down to the girl's level and explains how the boy must have felt when she pushed him. "Ah, a softer approach."

He slowly spins the woman around in the water, one full turn, and now she sees the girl and boy grown taller, older, smarter. They are standing in a conservatory classroom. The boy strums a classical guitar. The girl listens with a frown, disagreeing with him over the arrangement of the piece. Her hand shoots out— is she going to shove him again? Of course not. That is what children do. She lightly places it on his arm, having learned that the purpose of touch is to soothe, not to strike. He looks at her and smiles.

"Same students, same curriculum," says the old man. "Can you guess what the lesson is?"

"How to love one another?"

"Not such a riddle, after all."

She considers the love that slipped out of her grasp and into the skies one still summer night. "But why must I learn it on my own?"

"Who said that you were on your own? When have you ever been in a class without a teacher, a tutor? Nobody expected you to learn geometry or calculus on your own."

"I'm not certain I learned them at all."

The old man laughs. "Love is not as complicated as calculus. Don't make it so."

It may be less complicated, the woman thinks, yet what could be more brutal than the emotional mathematics of love? How it can shatter into fractions in an instant. How three minus two can equal zero. The cold, crisp precision with which division does its work, leaving behind a mere remainder of what was once whole.

She is not the only one who has watched love disappear from her life without warning, without reason. For ages, people have searched for the logic to this, for the answer to the unanswerable, the equation that would piece their fragmented life back together and give it meaning. They devised increasingly complex methods to solve the simple arithmetic of loss. They came up with algebra: the setting of bones, the reunion of fractured parts, the science of restoring what is missing. They created calculus, the study of how things change, from the very word meaning "stone" or "rock"—what better to describe death? "We will determine the value of the unknown," they said. "We will figure out the point of this pain." As if there were a reason, the woman says to herself. As if there were a point. As if all that intellectual activity were anything more than a baffled, broken mind running in circles. There is no science to subtraction, no formula to derive meaning from grief. Nothing can solve for loss. Loss has no solution.

She is exhausted. She has been working on this problem forever. To see the pattern behind the lifetimes is progress; to choose to keep repeating it is insanity. "I've had enough of an education," she decides. She will gladly agree to less knowledge if it means less suffering.

"You have more to learn," the old man tells her. "Master the material, then come back and teach it."

She remains unconvinced. If it is her decision to attend school, then it is her decision not to attend. And this school is so difficult. The lessons break her heart. The exams break her bones, and no math can mend them. What could ever make her come back day after day, body after body, lifetime after lifetime?

At that moment she happens to glance across the lake. On its banks rests a young schoolgirl with black braids against her head. She is drinking a cup of tea and delicately peeling a mandarin with her fingernail. Their eyes meet. The schoolgirl's eyes reflect something shining and gold: mountains, memories. A wool blanket lies on her lap. Its edges are unfinished, never finished, not until the warp wraps its arms around the weft one final time and refuses to let go. She waves at the woman, gives her a warm smile, and pats the grass next to her in an invitation to come sit. *Here you are, my little bird.*

LESSON 6

{

Duet

*H*ere you are, my little bird.

It's you! Are you really here?

Where else could I be?

You left me. How could you leave me?

I was a student. Now I am a teacher.

While I stay stuck in class.

Yes. I am so proud of you.

Proud? I am to blame for your death! Aren't you angry? Don't you regret ever meeting me, ever loving me?

Regret and *love* cannot share the same sentence.

They can if it is a death sentence.

You are not to blame. It was my choice.

I lit the candle. I gave it the power to strangle you. You were caught inside the attic. You had no choice, no chance.

Before there was so much as a flicker of the power, my higher self had already made its decision. You did not give strength to the flame. You gave it to me.

Why would you choose to leave me?

It was my gift to you.

Gifts are wrapped in paper and bows, not grief and tears.

Had I not left, you would not have left either. You would not have ventured from the shelter of our house into the darkness of the woods. You'd have stayed safe and small. You were an acorn: dormant, aching to grow. There is nothing wrong with being an acorn, except that you were meant to be the oak.

I am the oak?

An acorn must die. You don't see it that way, of course. You consider it a symbol of new life. Yet life is ferocious, it rips apart and discards all the acorn has ever known—its body, its identity, its very existence. Life doesn't arise from the seed; it kills the seed. But it grows the oak.

I am the oak . . .

Tragedies can make you sprout. Fire or gunfire, a self-inflicted death, a baby born without breath: the cause matters less than the consequence. Such things press against an acorn. They stretch it until the shell cannot contain it anymore. They break its home wide open. Do you allow them to turn you into the oak? Or do you swear off life altogether and decide to never become the tree?

I am the oak.

And I too am the oak. We are both becoming strong. We are both adding rings to our souls.

. . .

Are you really here?

Are *you* really here?

Are you really behind me?

Behind you, beside you, beyond you.

. . .

What is it like to die?

When I was a boy, my mother would wash my favorite blanket. She'd take it from the clothesline and hand it to me so I could bury my face in it. For a moment, my world was perfect soft-ness, freshness, warmth. It's like that, except now the moment does not end.

Death is not made of stone?

No, it's made of love.

Where are you now?

Outside of *where.*

But you still exist?

When you lie in bed at night and you dream, do you still exist?

Of course.

When you sleep, your spirit takes leave of the body. It flies. It joins me where I am. It speaks to God. It creates the world. You could say that it exists more than at any other time.

So death is like being asleep?

No. Life is like being asleep. Death is awakening.

. . .

What is it like to die?

To die is to learn the purpose of why you lived at all.

And why did you live?

I lived so that I could die, so that you could live.

How dreadful—you gave up your life for me?

It's like asking me to give up a breath for you. I have given a million others for much less noble purposes: a sigh, a cry, a call from the lungs. What's one more to spare, to breathe new life into you?

. . .

What is it like to die?

It's like being in a rear-end collision in a car. It's a push, a pop, a slight shock but nothing serious. It catches you off guard, or maybe you see it coming but can't get out of the way. Instead of being pushed forward into the street, you're pushed into a new dimension, one in which you can see the entire universe in all its clarity, in all its perfection.

How I wish I could see that.

You can. Open your eyes.

Does it hurt to die?

You're asking me if it hurts to become an angel? No more than it hurts the baby to become a child, the bud a blossom.

. . .

What is it like to die?

Here is the strangest thing. It isn't *like* anything. It's just know-ing more than you knew before. You've had that experience. Once you were a toddler who could barely speak, and then your vocabulary expands and you can describe all those things for which you never had the words. Or you're a musician who's finally figured out the fingering on a difficult piece, and it becomes simple to play the same passage with which you had struggled. When that happens, you change, but you don't stop existing! What stops existing is the level of consciousness that you have now grown out of.

So it's all a school, as the old man said? He showed me myself as a kindergartener, making my way up to conservatory. And, I assume, beyond that.

Yes. Clearly, a student does not die when she completes kindergarten. Her time as a kindergartener dies, I suppose you could say, but the student enters the first grade.

Why do we fear death so much, then? We don't grieve gradu-ations, we celebrate them.

For the same reason that the student may not wish to leave kindergarten. She gets to run around, to make art, to play with her friends. Why would she ever want to leave that? Well, she has to, because it has nothing left to teach her. So she moves on, she sees that her friends have done the same, and everything's fine again. Besides, it's kind of thrilling to be in a different class and have brand-new supplies, don't you think?

Here I have been mourning the body you wore, while you are excited for a back-to-school outfit.

Sometimes we get so big and strong that the old clothes no longer fit.

Don't you miss them, though? Don't you feel sad that they are no longer? I would.

Do you miss the bodies you wore in other lifetimes?

No.

That is your answer.

You tell me the body is unimportant, yet I loved your body. The curves of your calves, your smile, your mind. The delicacy with which your hands held the guitar, the urgency with which they held me. The sound of you sleeping; the bottom of your foot searching the sheets for the top of mine. How you would reach for me in the night, your eyes and your voice naked with need, your soul laid bare. The look that would cross your face, it was one of pleasure but also disbelief—disbelief that there could be such pleasure. And that it could belong to us.

Don't misunderstand me. The body is very important. Love is the *what*; the body is the *how*. Each one we've worn is a chapter in our story, its pages unfolding to the touch: a poem, a prayer book, a mystery, a love letter read so often that it becomes faded and creased. In the moonlight I would stroke the back of your neck and translate your skin into Braille. I'd stay up until morning savoring each word, lost in its tale of bruises and kisses, of battles that drew blood and scars.

What you say doesn't comfort me, for all you speak of is long gone. What good is a book if there is no one to read it? Do you know the pain those pages must feel? And why must our bodies be made so fragile, always leaving this world and taking everything along with them?

You have heard the legend of the genie, yes? A genie somehow becomes stuck inside a lamp, and if enough pressure is applied he escapes from it.

Sure, I know it.

Our bodies are the lamps. When death arrives, it is sufficiently strong to release us from our containers. Does the genie cease existing when he leaves the lamp? Quite the opposite. He becomes huge, ever-powerful; he can summon any desire from the ether. He arises from the smoke to stand by your side, yet you keep looking to the lamp! Don't mourn it, however beautiful and brilliant it may be. It contains the genie—one might even say it traps him—but when he breaks free from it, the magic begins.

. . .

Open your eyes now.

I can't.

You must.

. . .

You make death sound wonderful, while life—life is such misery. A husband that is no longer, a child that never was. And that's merely my sad little song. Everyone has his or her own tragedy. Multiply my pain by their pain, this lifetime by the last, by the next: there are thousands of permutations of sorrow. It's incalculable, exponential, too much to bear.

Why sing this song of sadness, when you can sing a love song instead?

I've lost all my love songs. I've forgotten how to play them, and how they sound.

You see the suffering in the world and insist upon multiplying the pain by the pain. Multiply the joy by the joy. Then you will understand the true meaning of *incalculable.* Pain may result from the lesson, but it is not the lesson. Growth is. Love is. Don't mistake a closet for a classroom.

I cannot find joy. Not anymore.

You can. It is what we are here to do. Do you know that in one lifetime, you came into this world simply to take pleasure in a summer night? Your sole purpose was to appreciate the artistry of July, to delight in her brushstrokes. What an advanced elective to take! And how beautifully you grasped the subject. The heat was hushed, the fireflies were floating lanterns, the garden you sat in glowed. The begonias were magic, and you were bewitched. Dusk fell and the evening stretched before you, softly sizzling with possibilities. Never mind the years and tears you shed before that night, or after; that life existed for that moment. Here is the thing: that could be every moment. It is your choice. This is the true meaning of reincarnation. We are not born over and over into a new body, but into a new moment. Open your eyes. In one day alone the world can explode with joy, and that is merely your sweet little song. Multiply that by every person, by every day, by every lifetime, and perhaps you are right: it is too much to bear.

. . .

If you chose not to stay here, why must I? Let me join you where you are.

You will. In the meantime, I join you where you are. The arms with which I hold you are made of breeze and rain, not flesh and bone; they are my arms nonetheless. I speak to you in coriander and clove, in cicada song. Every wildflower in your path is my footstep. When you come across a field of them, it means I have been dancing with you.

You say that you're around me, yet I can't see you.

You can if you open your eyes.

How I miss you.

Miss me? I have never left you, any more than I left you when we drifted into separate sleeps together in our bed.

And now we share the same sleep.

Sometimes I watch your dreams from afar, sometimes you invite me inside them. Either way I am with you every night, as I have always been, and I sing you to sleep, as I have always done.

Sing to me now.

No, now it is time for you to awaken, not to sleep.

. . .

The day is breaking. It is time to open your eyes.

I won't, for if I do, you'll disappear.

If you say so.

Don't leave me. Not again.

Open your eyes. It's time now. Open your eyes.

❧

Theme and Variation

"Open your eyes," the old man is saying. "It's time now. Open your eyes."

The woman does and finds his old self standing above her, the morning sun perched on his shoulder. All she wants to do is close them again, to be with her husband in that place where he is solid, not shadow. When sleep is the sole pleasure, why wake? When today is pain, why tomorrow? There is a hole in her heart where the dream had been. She longs to return to it, to dissolve in it, to disappear into her pasts. They hold what she wants. The future offers only something gray and misshapen.

Or does it? If she continues walking a road of misery, her endpoint naturally will be more of the same; every footstep follows the one before it. To move to the side, to turn around, to renounce the course and walk somewhere else entirely: this will change the terrain of tomorrow. There is no predestination, no destination. There are simply paths and possibilities, extending in infinite directions, waiting to be explored. The old man tells her so.

"We can go into the future?" she asks, incredulous.

"We can go into *a* future," he corrects her, his words leading her once more to the lake that holds all time.

. . .

The land is shell-shocked, pockmarked. The buildings are sleek and sanitized, the earth oozing and infectious. I live inside a hospital but I am safe, I am surgeon. The war is a mechanical, efficient scheduler, ensuring that no bed lies empty for long. It waits until we are asleep, then does its best work in the dark.

I place my hands on my patients to coax the toxins from within. The chemicals of warfare are difficult to remove from the bloodstream, the chemicals of fear even more so. But both can be fatal, and it is pointless to disarm one while allowing the other to gain ground.

Bodies are no longer sliced open, anesthetized, impregnated. We grow our babies on the outside now. I do not understand: If we can advance to the point of creating life, why can we not advance past the point of destroying it? We fight so hard to save lives, while others fight equally hard to end them. Humankind is scientifically progressive yet spiritually primitive, a dangerous mongrel.

Another doctor stands beside me. His hair is as red as the birthmark on his cheek. My hands rest on the patient's body, his hands above mine. Our light combines to make her cells kindle and spark. I love him quietly, fraternally, the same way I love my patients, the same way I love even those who unleash their venom upon the earth, although they will not allow the love to enter them. They are terrified of the damage it might do.

One of my patients is a mere infant, too small to compete with poison. War has taken over her tiny life, and now it's come to claim her death. As a physician, I've been trained to accept that the human body will occasionally do battle with itself. But when the human mind goes awry—when it considers a newborn baby worthy of attack—well, what training could prepare someone for this?

There is also a boy, not yet five years old, whose trauma is written all over his face. I use my hands to erase its words, to replace it with

a new story, one in which the only soldiers are
made of plastic and make-believe. Whenever
possible, I sneak into his room and sit with
him so that he can relax into sleep. I can see
his heart without having to look. It is pastel
and pure. I never saw the eyes of the unborn
daughter I lost to the fire, but they are the same,
they are his. I know this, too, without having
to look.

It is a struggle to ascend from the water; the hopelessness
of the future weighs the woman down like a rock. For a brief
moment she considers letting it drown her. Her husband has
assured her that death is not bleak, but no one can promise the
same of life.

"War evolves into something quite sophisticated. Then again,
so does healing." The old man points at her harp. "It was wise
to bring your talents with you."

"I was a doctor, not a musician."

"What's the difference? Only the instrument of healing. The
bodies you play are made of tissues and nerves, instead of silk
and willow. You tune cells rather than strings. You make both
vibrate with harmony. You already know how to create white
light with music. Soon you will do it without."

The woman spreads her arms across the lake, smoothing its
surface, feeling in its depths for the frightened boy for whom
she had tried to create a fairy tale. She reaches, she searches, yet

her fingers cannot hold on to the slippery spirit. With each life-time it seems to elude her more, to swim farther away, not even her child any longer. Her patient, but somebody else's child.

"You were the mother," the old man says, "just in a differ-ent way."

"And the little infant? She was so familiar, though I could not place her. If it wasn't the same soul as the child I lost in this life, then who was it?"

The mare lifts its head at the question, looks into the woman's eyes, waits for the recognition to dawn.

.   .   .

The woman says, "I don't care much for the future."

"Then change it," says the old man.

"How?"

"What do you mean, how? It isn't a riddle. Compose a new one."

> The war lumbers on. The infant girl dies, as does the young boy. I cannot save them. I have nothing to offer; my light is brittle and cold. The windows of the hospital are sealed and the toxins cannot reach us, though I feel that they must have. What else could explain this strange pain inside me, slowly shutting me down? My colleagues volunteer their help. I don't accept it.

Why should I live, just to watch children die?
They do not let me place my hands on the sick.
My touch is too leaden. It would leave them
susceptible to shock, to an infection of sorrow.

The old man shakes his head. "Wrong direction."

The war lumbers on. The patients respond to
my medicine. One night, the red-haired doctor
places his hands on mine instead of above them.
Outside our windows people are killing. Inside
our walls people are dying. But I—I have just
been brought to life. To think that he has been
by my side the entire time; I never knew to look
for the love buried underneath war. The infant
remains alive, although not for much longer.
The little boy calls me Mother.

"What does happiness sound like to you? Why insist on a
war at all? Are you so scared to be at peace?"

I place my hands above the little boy. His blood
is strong and clean, like the air that pours past
the unsealed windows. I try to look outside the
windows yet it seems that I cannot, for flowers obscure my view. Oh, to find flowers again!
The red-haired doctor is beside me, and I kiss

the birthmark on the cheek where the fire once
touched. I love him in spite of it. I love him
because of it. He asks if I am ready. Ready for
what? To go outside, of course. The world is
lush and green and fertile, and the only beds
I tend to belong to the roses. The boy sprawls
across my lap. I uproot a buttercup and place
it under his chin, and he glows because he has
never known a day of terror in his life. The
infant girl has grown into health, into childhood. She runs through the fields, running,
running, spinning and dancing and throwing
her arms up with delight. Her legs are small
and bowed with youth, little wishbones. She
falls over and laughs, she stands up, she is off
again and running toward the sun, never catching it, always trying—

The woman is buoyant. She could not stay underwater if
she tried. She has not lost her unborn daughter; she has found
her, in a little boy who shines with buttercups and wonder.
Her mare is there, as is her husband. Always he is there. The
glassy waters of the lake are a prism that refracts him everywhere she looks. How senseless it is to grieve one body when
he will be given to her in countless more. Death is not loss; it
is simply the opportunity to love one another in a thousand
different forms.

She had been right. There is no future without him. But those words mean something else now.

This had been her fear: that, despite having returned to her again and again in the past, perhaps he would finally decide not to. That he would touch the burns on his cheek and find them too painful—that he would find her too painful.

This had been her shame: the wounds did not begin with the fire. More than once she'd harbored snakes inside her—harsh words, thoughtless words, various meannesses in all their slimy forms—that had slipped past her lips to bite him. How can the same mouth be used to kiss and to harm? She had lit the candle out of love so that her husband could make his way through the night. She had lit the candle and she had slammed the door, and what resulted, though tragic, was accidental. The real injuries are already forgiven. They have been forgiven over and over.

She nicks him with a curt remark. He shoots a spear tipped with betrayal straight through her. She strikes the match; he goes down in flames. Lovers learn a hundred ways to hurt, to scar—with weapons and with words (or the lack thereof). Their arsenals are plentiful, personal. They wage drawn-out wars and then reenact them. Yet even the most embittered will come to find themselves looking at one another through windows overflowing with flowers. Easily the woman and her husband could have turned enemies, what with all the wounds they had inflicted. Instead, they became each other's doctor.

Here she is again in his arms in the future, in all futures, as though death had not disentangled them. Centuries pass, bodies pass, to no lasting effect. It is like being held by him as she falls asleep, separating during the night, and waking in the morning to discover herself once more in his embrace. To stay stubbornly in a dream and in a past is to close her eyes to the sunlight that lies in wait. Tomorrow, she now understands, is not a thing to escape from, to cast aside, to wish away. It is the thing you run toward, spinning, dancing, your arms outstretched with delight, never catching, always trying.

≀

Dotted Note

*T*he old man says, "You have seen the past."

"Yes," the woman replies.

"You have seen the future."

"Yes."

"They have brought you some comfort."

"Oh yes."

"Good, now forget them both. They don't exist. They never have."

. . .

"There is one moment: now. Time implies more. There is no more. There is one place: here. You are here—now." The old man pauses to consider the lake and all who occupy it. "How can time be an illusion, if you are inside it? How can the lake not be real if you are within its waters, and you are real? Or are you?"

He lifts his arms up and to the sides in a swoop of a motion, gathering the entirety of the lake and condensing it into a single droplet that rests on the palm of his hand. "Here is time," he says, then lightly blows on the bead until it floats away, a bubble. "And there it goes. Yet here you still are, outside it, alive. How can that be?"

He spreads his arms wide and the lake appears before them again, as calm and clear as ever. Here; gone. Here; gone. The tide of time, drawing her into its depths, releasing her to rest on its shores, depositing its riches at her feet. The softly swelling wave that takes her nowhere, that takes her everywhere.

The woman stares into the bottomless waters that have held her husband, her child, her self. She looks into its face and sees her own: placid, eternal. It is not the enemy, not the thief, not the monster. It is merely that which lends her the six hundred million breaths of a life. She descends into it, and time surrounds her; she emerges and it evaporates from her. Were the old man to dissolve the lake once and for all, the birdlike creatures that dot its banks would not disappear along with it. They would simply sail away on those wings made of mercury and memory, their feathers growing streaked with silver and flecked with cloud as they flew off in formation toward some new nest.

But if time is no more permanent and no less delicate than a bubble afloat, then what of everything that's experienced inside it? Is that, too, as fragile, as fleeting?

She swirls her finger in the water, thinking out loud. "Time is one of the things we come here to learn about, then."

"Sure, if you're a physicist."

"It's not an important lesson?"

"Less the lesson than the vehicle through which it is conveyed—the textbook, but not its subject."

A lake of time, a book of words: the contents, he knows, are more important than the container. Both allow for alchemy. Both leave their fingerprints on the soul. A book belongs inside and beyond time and space. A reader can dip into its pages and swim in its words, put it down, walk away, come back to it years later, come back to it even after its author has died. It alters the consciousness and the heart, yet its effects do not vanish when its cover is closed, when it is returned to the shelf, when its events are purely fictional and never physical. The book itself may be destroyed, its words erased or struck from the page—but not from the reader. The material world is the same. Reality can disperse with the wave of the old man's hand, the illumination of the woman's mind. The medium comes and goes. The insight remains.

He says to her, "You think that there is one of you and many times. One stable, enduring self, and yesterday, next month, eight hundred years ago, August sixteenth, childhood, nine o'clock in the morning, autumn, 480 B.C. To you, time is a line—a time-line—that the same one person walks day after day, in the same one direction, from newborn to old and gray. What if, instead, there are many selves and one time? If the you of a few seconds ago and the you of a few seconds from now are two completely separate selves? The you of yesterday, the you of last autumn and the next, the you of eight hundred years ago, the you as a child and the you of old age: infinite you's existing concurrently, developing simultaneously. Then there is no line, only a single plot point. And that one single point, that one dot, is limitless and contains all the immeasurable variations of you within it."

As he speaks, something is happening to her eyes, for what they are seeing is no longer an elderly man but one whose wrinkles have smoothed, whose body has lengthened into that of a young adult and then compressed into that of a small boy. She blinks to bring him back into focus. He places his hand atop hers and says, "It's all right. Let it go."

Her question is earnest, her confusion profound. "If there is only the dot—which contains every life that I have ever lived and will ever live—and a billion of me exist all at once, then when was I born? And when do I die?"

The smile that he gives her is toothless and wide, the kind shared by babies and old men alike.

. . .

The old man waves his arms in front of the woman's face, and once more she sees the steppes, the warrior, the blood. She moans. She cannot bear this again.

He is both sympathetic and insistent. "Change what you did."

"I can't change the past!"

"Says who?"

"Something that has already happened cannot be changed. That doesn't make any sense."

"In a timeline, it makes no sense. When everything is happening all at once, nothing could be easier. There is no past. You with the knife on the steppes, you with the mare by the lake, you with the patients in the war: they are all you *right now*. They are all you right now in the big dot. Touch one and you touch them all." He bends to pick a pebble from the ground, then tosses it into the center of the lake. The ripple radiates outward in concentric circles, finally reaching her feet, as well as the bare feet of the warrior. His are clasped by a young mother and her child, who stare up at his knife, at his terrible grin.

The warrior's hands hold the knife, the woman's hold history: it feels just as heavy, just as dangerous. "What do I do?" she asks, and the old man says, "What do you want to do?"

Look at me, she commands the warrior, no closer to him than a thousand years, no farther than a thought. He turns around in bewilderment, unsure of the source of the voice. His eyes lock on hers and a sizzle runs through them both: the strange recognition of one's own soul in the body of another. To her surprise, her greatest compassion is directed not toward the victims but toward someone else altogether. *It will be all right*, she tells him. *We will be all right. You didn't know any better, but you are learning.* It occurs to her that some future self may be watching her lie in the grass as her house and husband burn, sending her the same mental message.

The warrior stops cold. Compassion? What is this thing which dulls his knife? He stares at the woman. Her eyes shine with the answer. He lays the weapon on the ground and backs away from the mother and child. The mother realizes what is happening, what is not happening. She clutches the child to her chest and off they run, mice escaping the talons of a hawk.

The woman witnessing this scene follows the mother in her mind. She sees the mother rush inside her home into the waiting arms of her spouse. Her words describe making death's acquaintance. Her face tells the real story: *All I could think of was you, of the wintry night of our first kiss, your lashes bejeweled with snowflakes, your touch turning me into spring.*

Her spouse exhales his relief. The burden that lifts is indescribable, inaccessible, no longer his. When the warrior had emptied his wife's and child's bellies, his own had filled with hatred and despair. This time, the weapon set aside and the family unharmed, he will not have to swallow his resentment, will never know its sharp taste and how it slices the tongue. It is as if the woman is watching an artist stand before a pencil sketch, erasing portions of a picture she has made and, with a careful hand, drawing something more refined.

That mother becomes mother many times more. Her child and his siblings grow and swell with their own families and give birth to generations that throb with life and flourish and expand and spread across the land and spill over into the oceans and onto boats and into new continents and build thriving cities and civilizations and fill every last inch of the earth with the children of their children, all of whom are born from the moment when the warrior laid down his knife.

Touch one and you touch them all.

For the warrior, the moment is one not of birth but of death—the death of the warrior in him. A new part grows in its place. Now he knows of compassion, though not what to do with it. On whom can he test the concept? No one is around except a lonely saxaul tree, bloomless and bare. It will have to do. He tends to it, waters its soil, speaks to it of sunlight and shade. The tree has never known flowers. The warrior teaches it flowers. Under his care, its roots strengthen and multiply. It makes a forest of itself so that the animals can take shelter and the nomads can take wood. Compassion. The warrior has given it life; now it will return the favor unto him. It spots a hungry sparrow hiding in a shrub and drops its seeds to feed it. A seed swallowed cannot grow, but the tree is willing to forgo its own future for that of the warrior. Like the tree, the sparrow can offer him companionship. Unlike the tree, it can also offer him song.

The warrior has never seen such a bird before. He listens every morning for its concert. The two trade melodies, learn the rhythms of each other's days. Bloodthirst turns into songthirst, the warrior into a musician.

The bird is new to wings. It has spent lifetimes as breezes and currents; now it must learn how to navigate them. One day it will fly with legs instead of feathers, and the wind that it once was will propel its hooves and whip through its mane. And the warrior, sitting on its back in the shape of a woman, will feel this wind too as it sweeps through her hair, as it weaves through her harp, playing the songs of the sparrow on its strings.

· · ·

Compassion is not an act of goodwill but the cascade that the act creates.

The woman pictures the warrior not backing away from the mother and the child and the violent impulse. As she does, the sequence of events halts and reverses: entire generations lying fallow, a lonely spouse choking to death on a piece of anger lodged in his throat, the warrior knowing neither sparrow nor song. "What if I hadn't killed them and instead raped the mother in front of her child, or stolen all that they owned, or just yelled at them and gone on my way? Would that have changed everything as well?"

"Not so radically," the old man tells her, "for each of those actions is born of cruelty, and cruelty is cruelty, the degree being of less consequence than the substance itself. You don't need to save or spare a life to create this chain reaction, though. It can begin with something as quiet as giving seeds to a hungry sparrow, or as easy as falling into the loving arms of your family." The cascade, hearing his words, flows forward once more. He watches it with a wistful expression. "If only people understood how the earth turns on a kindness."

The woman's thoughts also flow ahead. She could lay down a knife and alter the course of a life. Could she do the same with a match? "If we can change what has been done, then I can catch the candle that burned down my house, or never light it at all."

"Yes," he says, "although you do not need to. There is a world in which you have already done those things. There is a world in which the power does not die, and no candle falls for you to catch. And in those worlds, your husband and daughter are very much alive."

. . .

The old man kneels down and plucks a daisy from its bed of grass. Each petal surrounding the yellow heart—and to the woman, there seem to be multitudes—bears a single drop of dew.

"Make a decision," he tells her, "and the universe splits in two. In one universe you have chosen the first option, in the other the second. Take an action in the daughter universes, and they too divide. All the universes occur at the same time, parallel and yet worlds apart. All of them result in unique outcomes—or maybe not. All of them are your reality, one no less than the other."

The woman has seen firsthand how a world can splinter, how it can divide a life into loneliness, a wife into widow. The before and the after, the source and the shard. But to inhabit them both? It cannot happen. The original one, the one with the happiness, lies broken in too many pieces.

"Say that you are getting dressed one morning, and you put on a gold locket." The old man removes a petal from the daisy and hands it to her. The dewdrop on it is like a crystal ball. Inside it, she watches herself fastening the clasp of the necklace. "Or you decide to wear nothing around your neck but perfume." He gives her another petal, and in this one she sees that her throat is bare.

The woman returns them both to him. Two different universes? All that has changed is her jewelry.

"Look closer," he says.

She examines the first petal. She sees herself wearing the locket, entering a market, waiting to purchase coriander and clove. The shopkeeper notices the gold on her neck. It makes his eyes gleam. "My grandmother wore a necklace like yours," he says to her. "My grandfather gave it to her on the day they were wed. She kept a lock of his hair inside it, and one night, when she tucked me into bed, she let me touch it. It was the closest I ever came to holding him." The woman lingers at the register, moved to be invited inside this memory. They share a smile. She thanks the shopkeeper, leaves the store, turns right, and heads toward home.

She turns her attention to the second petal. Now she is locketless, entering the market, waiting to make her purchase. The shopkeeper nods at her, says nothing. She leaves the store and turns right, which happens, in this scenario, to be a few minutes earlier than it had been in the previous one, and which also happens to be the precise moment when a bus climbs the curb and pins her under its wheels.

"Rather dramatic way to make your point," she huffs.

The old man laughs and hands her another petal.

She sees herself lying underneath the wheels. With enough effort, she could try to pull herself out from under them, but that would require more than she has. She gives up. Her life flows away along with her blood.

The woman throws the petal onto the grass. The mare, curious, sniffs the world tossed aside.

A petal: She tries to pull herself from under the bus. An ambulance arrives to finish the job. It whisks her into an operating room, where the surgeons sew her back together. Her health restored, she is discharged from the hospital. She walks out the main doors, a doctor walks in, they collide. The doctor helps her to her feet. He looks at her. He cannot look away. She doesn't let go of his hand. They will marry, initiate each other into the secret society of love, die decades later after having mastered its countless mysteries.

Another petal: Her health restored, she is discharged from the hospital. She walks out the main doors, a doctor walks in, they collide. The doctor helps her to her feet. He looks at her. He looks away. "Watch where you're going," he mutters. She lets go of his hand.

A petal: The doctor who has passed love by moves to an isolated cabin in the country. Unconnected, unfulfilled, he does not know what to do with his empty hours, and so he fills them with liquor. He drinks himself to an early death.

Another petal: The doctor who has passed love by moves to an isolated cabin in the country. Unconnected, unfulfilled, he applies his empty hours to his work, and so he discovers the cure for cancer. Millions of people who wouldn't otherwise exist now do.

A petal: A cancer patient does not receive the cure in time and dies.

Another petal: A cancer patient receives the cure in time and lives.

A petal: The patient who once had cancer and now does not gets dressed one morning and puts on a gold locket, or wears nothing around her neck but perfume.

For each petal the old man plucks, a new one immediately springs up in its place. The flower he holds is only one in a never-ending garland of daisy chains. He drapes them around the woman's neck and her arms, covering her in the impossible blossoms. "That's just what happens when you turn right. Had you turned left . . ." he says, and there are daisies, daisies everywhere, each petal one of innumerable worlds revolving around a shared sun.

"Many me's, one time," she replies, and her mind splits open alongside the universe.

• • •

The woman rests on the grass. The mare lies at her feet, the harp in her hands. She opens *Music Lessons* and reads, expecting to find a new piece to practice yet finding only a basic command:

PLAY A NOTE.

Play a note? she thinks. Before, she could barely wrap her mind and her fingers around the complicated melodies in the book, and now it has become a primer?

THIS IS AN EXERCISE IN COMPOSITION, NOT PERFORMANCE.

Still skeptical, she plucks the A string. The sound skips across the lake and reaches the silvery spirits on the banks, who become motionless upon hearing it. It reminds them of sadness. They had forgotten about sadness. Without human bodies, without human lives, sorrow is unheard of; tears, like all water, dry as soon as they lift themselves from the lake. The music makes it materialize once more. It passes through them like a ghost—invisible, insidious—and haunts them with feelings laid to rest long ago. In this way, sound is super-natural. It resurrects the heart, brings memories back from the dead.

Like these saddened souls, the universe has just been torn apart. In one, the woman plays the D note, which makes the listeners weep. In another she plays both notes together, and in another she can't decide which to choose and so plays nothing, and the universe splits anyway because to not make a decision is to make a decision.

She plays another note. And another. And the universe splits on . . .

And on . . .

And on . . .

THAT IS JUST A NOTE. IMAGINE A WHOLE SONG.

THAT IS JUST A SONG. IMAGINE A WHOLE LIFE.

Her mind catches sight of infinity but, once glimpsed, it skitters away. Perhaps the instruction is not as basic as she had believed. Perhaps the entire symphony lies inside the single note.

THERE IS A THEORY THAT EXPLAINS HOW ALL THESE UNIVERSES COME TO BE.

She reads on while continuing to play, her fingertips stroking the harp, conjuring forth new realms.

IT IS CALLED STRING THEORY.

. . .

Music is a universe of sound, constantly expanding and dividing. Compositions are carved into movements and passages. A half note branches off into quarter notes, sixteenth notes—the same tone, yet held for a different duration, a different effect. A harmony of multiple notes, a counterpoint of multiple melodies, an orchestra of multiple instruments: separate spheres, playing in parallel.

A composer must make order out of this hopeless profusion of noise. To play every note at once—one big, all-encompassing dot—would produce chaos. To play none would produce silence. But to space them out artfully on a staff of time: that would produce a masterpiece.

And so the composer splits the piece into measures and meter. The notes are held tight within bar lines, told when to ring out and when to die out, when to attack and when to decay. They are given finite boundaries. *You will last for eight breaths, and no more.* To them, time is fixed; to the composer, it is fluid. She could speed it up, slow it down, change duple meter to triple meter or a march to a waltz. She knows that the beauty lies not in how long the note lasts, but in the sound that it makes while it does.

Maybe, the woman thinks, our composer has done the same with us. Lest eternity seem too long and infinity too loud, she imposes measures on our existence, divides it into years, generations, incarnations. We count beats and birthdays. We emerge from the silence, and we fade back into it. This is not a punishment or a curse, any more than it is to assign a time signature to a song. After all, if there is no beat, how can there be a dance?

She does not do this to make us suffer. She does this to make us music.

. . .

"There's a world in which we are having this conversation, and a world in which we aren't," the woman says.

"And the world in which we are having this conversation arises from the world in which your husband dies, for would we have ever met had you not left your house in mourning and ventured into the forest? That's a trick question, by the way." The old man sits beside the woman on the grass, letting his gaze wander across time. "What if your husband had lived, and one afternoon you were doing the laundry, and you went to collect it from the clothesline when a wild boar ran up and snatched his yellow sweater from the line, and you went running after it because that was his favorite sweater, and you chased the boar clear through the forest until you finally caught up with it, and when you grabbed the sweater from its snout you saw that it was covered in dirt and hair and so you decided to give it a rinse in the nearby lake, which was, of course, the lake of time, and there I was sitting at its edge, waiting for you? There are certain people you must meet, whether by grief or by boar or some other proxy of fate. Of course, what you do with that meeting is up to you."

This must be so, thinks the woman, for when did she ever not encounter her husband in the waters of time? If she can turn left or turn right and find him, dive into her dreams or into the lake and find him, disguise herself in the body of a hunter or the body of a lotus and still find him—then loss is nothing more than an illusion, a riddle of one's own creation.

Her blood quickens with excitement. There is a universe in which he escapes the smoke before it smothers him. In which the kitchen door shuts silently. In which it does not, but she sees the flame and rushes to right the fallen candle, the fallen family. In which he and the child live, or he lives and the child does not, or the child lives and he does not, or they live and the woman does not. In untold dimensions they are together, yet her awareness remains firmly fixed inside one in which they are apart. What if she chose to inhabit another? Is that even feasible? Here comes infinity again, emerging from the shadows of her mind to make its presence known.

The old man sweeps his hands over the clouds. The sun falls through his fingers, and the blue turns into black. The moon and constellations hurry to assume their positions in the darkness. "Suppose that a single star, surrounded by billions of its brothers, presumed itself to be the sole one in all the heavens." At his words, everything disappears apart from a tiny, blinking orb, meaningless in the vast nothing of space. "You know that it is mistaken, for you have seen the others. Just because they may not be visible to the star does not mean that they are not there. If it were to realize that it is but one of a galaxy . . ." he says, and the night becomes floodlit once more.

The woman is made mute with possibilities, watching the stars swirl in the skies, in the old man's eyes. By the time she perceives them, by the time she speaks their names, some have already extinguished themselves. The polite ones quietly turn off the lights. Others, aching for obliteration, collapse into a black hole deeper than any she has known, only to find themselves streaming down the Milky Way to be born again as new stars, or as lilacs, or as her. She sits at some point in the future, which does not even exist, beholding those beautiful bodies that have long since ceased to be. It is light after death, life after death.

Time is not such a difficult puzzle. Its solution is always right here. And death is not an indomitable obstacle, nor is it made of stone. That is just the perspective of someone who has sealed herself inside a cave of pain. She almost has to laugh. The sky has been showing her the answer all along. There is no end!

Even the most massive beings in the cosmos could not snuff out life. What had made her think that she held such power?

The old man takes her hands in his. As he does, the earth trembles and divides beneath them: a decision has just been made.

"I suppose that, in one world, we leave you," she says.

He smiles and replies, "It's time." The lake recedes into a shroud of fog, and then he, too, disappears inside it, leaving the woman and the mare standing by themselves, all alone in the clearing. She nudges the mare, leading it in the direction opposite the forest from which they had arrived. There is no going back now.

And, strangely, this does not scare her.

"What is there to fear?" she says to the mare, who treads gingerly on the fallen leaves, reluctant to set forth on its injured leg. The woman has no such hesitation. Her feet and mind race ahead. "You are immortal. I have seen it! My husband, I have found you too. The king and queen told me I could not look back at you, and it is true: I cannot look back. And I cannot look forward. There is only here, there is only now, and you are here, I know that now. They were not warning me. They were teaching me." She is giddy, her words are airborne. They float upward to the stars, which hear them a trillion years ago. "There is no such thing as death, and I can never die."

No sooner has she finished speaking these words than she steps on a snake, it bites her, and she dies.

≀

Overtones

A beach. An ocean as silver as her spirit. Cloud sinking into sea, sea ascending to become cloud: the same water, flowing back and forth between bodies. The waves break, then piece themselves back together. The skeletons of snails are reborn as shells. The skeletons of shells are reborn as sand. Death and birth, ebb and flow, an endless tide.

The woman stands on the shoreline. The surf nibbles her toes. Her feet are little, her footprints shallow. She looks down at them. They are her own, yet they belong to a young girl—one of many years ago. She is inside a memory of which she has no memory, though it has been here all along, silent and patient, awaiting her return.

The sea is warm and soothing, as is the sound of her mother calling her name. It crosses the shore and the water to reach the ears of the girl, decades and death to reach the ears of the woman. The mother watches the approach of a wave that swells with fury and threatens to drown the girl in its seething anger. "Come, come," she cries to her daughter, concerned. But the girl is watching a seagull evict and swallow a hermit crab, she is sifting through sand, she is invoking the magical names of the shells—*angel wings, bleeding tooth, lion's paw, baby's ear*—and nothing can move her from this moment.

The wave closes in. Her father rushes over, scoops her up, and lifts her in the air, so high that she thinks she can cup her hands around the sun. She shrieks with the thrill of flight and of father. He is backlit; she cannot see his face. The face does not matter, the face will change anyway. What matters is what she does see: the silhouette of pure love, that thing which lifts you into the clouds.

The wave hurls itself upon them. It fails to grab hold of her and recedes with a frustrated roar. The father lowers her. She too is like the tide, rising and receding. She burrows deep into his arms, tasting salt on her lips, listening to the strident chants of the sea and the gulls. This, the woman understands, is why her soul has dipped into time and body: to experience the exhilaration of bare feet in the surf, of falling deliriously into the arms of someone you adore, of a happiness so strong that it must escape the body in laughter or explode the body in pieces.

Now she feels it once again. Now she knows.

Now she knows that heaven is not found somewhere else but in those moments when there is nowhere else. That music is the sound of her mother's voice calling her closer, and no strings could ever replicate its splendor. That her mother, who had cherished the woman's father for numberless lifetimes, had in this one purposely chosen a body that would decompose while still alive, while still young. That this was an opportunity, not a tragedy; that his taking care of her was a reflection of her love for him, not his love for her. Where better for him to discover the beauty of unconditional love than amid the ugliness of disease? How better to refine his heart, to turn it into something both stronger and softer? And when time finally came to collect his last breath, he found himself, just as his daughter now does, on this very beach, his wife whole and healthy once more, all the illness and pain and loss erased, as if they never happened— and perhaps they never did—for here they are together again, she is windswept and beaming, he is lifting his baby girl up as far as she can go, and then he is rising too, he is soaring, farther, farther, he is somewhere near the sun, or is he the sun?

Now she knows that her mother, and her own husband, and her unborn child gave up their bodies out of love, and that they are not the only ones. The snails do it, so hermits and humans can delight in their shells. The shells do it, to carpet the beach, turn sharpness into sand. She knows that the crab is a master of love, willingly surrendering itself to the gull to sustain it, to nourish it. That the crab's eyes shine as it tells the gull, "I lived so that I could die, so that you could live." That what she calls *crab* is no less than godstuff packed into a small, sideways body; that what she calls *death* is merely the time it spends in between shells. While others stand over its old home and weep, the crab rejoices to be rid of the weight upon its back. While others fixate on the empty husk and grieve, the crab streaks wildly across the sky, naked and lustrous and limitless.

Now she knows that the wave approaches in love, not anger. That its entire life—its birth, its swell, its death—is orchestrated to bring the girl into her father's arms, to give them this dance together. For if it did not make itself quite so tall, would her father have lifted her quite so high? How else is she to touch the clouds? She knows that it would travel the oceans for this purpose, for this moment. And when the wave is needed no longer, it releases its body unto the shore and dies with a glorious sigh of satisfaction, and the sea enfolds it in its arms and whispers, "Welcome home."

Now she knows—now she remembers—that to die is nothing more than to be born to this knowledge: that everything, all along, has always been love.

{

Lullaby

*T*he recollection of the beach fades away, for it too has served its purpose. The gulls disperse. The crab fizzles out like a firework. The sea parts to reveal a forest of trees, which huddle around the lifeless human body lying on the ground.

From above, the woman stares down at herself. Her hair spills onto the mossy floor, the earth her pillow. Her skin turns chameleon, flashing all shades—red, purple—until it finally lands on gray. The mare paces back and forth, limping, frantic. It has lost her too many times over the centuries. It knows death; it refuses it. The mare grows increasingly frenzied. The woman does not. She giggles to herself. This is what people are so afraid of? Everyday life is far more menacing. Death is nothing more than a house cat; life is the lion, with the deafening roar, the jaws and claws.

She has died! She has gone ahead and done it. Always she'd wondered what it would be like, what form it might take, and to have the definitive answer is satisfying. Snakebite, of all things! She had danced around so many different possibilities, never recognizing this one as her rightful partner, waiting to lead her through her last steps. She had tended to picture herself shriveled in a bed, her face devoured by age, her life exiting in a polite breath. But hadn't her husband taught her that death can announce itself in unimaginable ways, and with dazzling pyrotechnics to boot?

She looks down at herself for the first time, the only time. It is an odd sensation, like passing an unexpected mirror and thinking, for a moment, that her reflection is someone else. She had always felt an attachment to her body; how could she not, it being so relentlessly present? Yet now that she is minutes from it, miles from it, she feels nothing. She is the oak, and the oak does not prostrate itself, weeping, before the acorn that has just burst open.

The mare neighs its panic. The woman does not hear it—she sees it. Every time the mare opens its mouth, small cubes tumble out and build upon one another, forming a chain of blocks that stretch toward the woman, who is already so far away. She touches the block nearest her, feels its fabric. It is made of fear, its edges sharp and serrated. The chain grows longer and sparser as the mare recedes from sight. Although it saddens her to see her friend in distress, she is grateful to distance herself from such misery. She wonders if her husband thought the same as he wended his own way upward—if he witnessed her lying in the grass, her screams reaching up to him in blocks made of knives and broken glass, and felt nothing but relief to leave behind the pain of being alive.

The night sky envelops the woman, forming an ocean around her in which she swims. The stars stream past her like silver minnows. She does not float so much as melt. She becomes smaller and smaller until she is the merest piece of herself, no more than the froth borne along the waves. To throw off the tight confines of the body, to become as nothing and as everything as the tiniest speck of sea foam, to dissolve into the water and become not the diver or even the dive but that which is dived into—*Oh, my mare,* she thinks, *if only you could know what freedom truly is.* How selfish she had been in her grief, to summon her husband back from this, to shackle him. Why would he leave this?

He would leave this for her.

She continues condensing, turning from person to particle to nothing. She has no thoughts, for she has no self. She is the speed of light and she is the light. And as she becomes the light, she becomes aware of being the light, and of the sea that surrounds her, whose darkness must mean that it is other. With this notion, her consciousness forms once more. The pieces of her are put back together. How long was she insentient? A million years, a mayfly's life. The staccato and the sustain.

The ocean compresses and compacts her, molds a body around her light. It throbs with pressure, contracting and relaxing in a primal, percussive rhythm. The tempo accelerates. Each contraction pushes her farther, toward what she does not know. All she can make out is a sound, which grows stronger as it grows closer: the unmistakable music of a child's laughter.

The light and the warmth and the school of stars swimming alongside the woman are so beautiful that she starts sobbing. Now she understands the real reason why newborns cry. And if their death day is in fact a birthday, then their birthday must also be a death day: a farewell to the ocean, a lifelong separation from the stars. This, too, makes them cry.

Everything then explodes into white-blue fire, blinding in the most pleasurable way. The woman cannot see. She does not know whether she has ceased to exist or begun to exist. The nurses grab her by the shoulders. The ocean empties itself of her and unfolds back into the night sky. She is delivered into a pair of arms that have been waiting all this time to hold her. The laughter she heard before bubbles up and spills over into kisses on her face. She blinks. The eyes that meet hers glitter with adoration.

They are the eyes of her daughter.

She had never seen them, not in this lifetime. The daughter had reversed direction, drifted upstream instead of down, raised herself from time's depths rather than submerging in them. But the woman had once held the daughter's body inside hers, and she knew it as well as she did her own. Besides, recognition is a sense that lies beyond sight.

In the light they behold each other, and they are both each other's child, and each other's mother.

"Love," the woman says, and the word, the first she has ever spoken to her child, comes barreling out with force from behind a dam of grief.

"Love," the child replies, swaddling the woman with its cashmere softness.

"Loss," the woman says, curling her fist around the child's fingers, feeling them inside hers.

The child nods as she rests her palms on the woman's belly, that sweet, velvet house.

The woman lowers her eyes and says, "Guilt." Her voice breaks as she turns her head and adds, "Shame." The disintegration of her child has been an unsolvable riddle. Why would death not spare something so pure? Her husband had at least lived out some of his days. Her child had lived none and could not be to blame. So where else could the blame lie?

The child knows that it is no riddle, no accident; that she is the cause and not the casualty. She gently lifts the woman's chin. The woman looks up at her daughter—how could she have pulled away from her, even for a second? What strength there is in shame, to turn your face from someone you love— and watches as time unfurls in her eyes. The woman sees herself with her husband in a bed glowing with moonlight. Sees how a kiss opens the floodgates, grants permission for one soul to enter the other. Hears the song she sings in his ear, the song he sings inside her; how their bodies are exquisite instruments that, with the breath, the lips, the fingertips, can too be made to sing; how, when played together, the music they make is written in the key of God. Their bodies remain in bed while their spirits rise, coming close to a silvery being who stands outside a lake, so close that they can almost touch her. Instead, the music does. The being becomes enchanted with it, knowing that the melody is meant for her. It beckons her into the water. She slips inside and glides through time, searching for the source of her song.

She enters time but does not yet belong to it. She enters the mother but does not yet belong to her, either. Momentum builds within the lake. Time takes shape, grows faster. So does her body. The current picks up speed. It sweeps the being along, flowing ever forward to reach the open ocean of the night sky. There it leaves her to swim among the stars with the other babies-to-be, all those willing to exchange their wings for wisdom.

The woman had always known of the cord tethering baby to mother, though not of the cord tethering baby to sky. This is how the beings shuttle between the stars and the wombs, from one temporary home to another. They flit along the cord until they are born, entering and exiting their mothers each night, as diaphanous as dreams. Meanwhile, the mothers work hard in their sleep, silently knitting the babies' bones together, embroidering a pattern of vessels and veins, stitching the cells. Sometimes the material snags, the seams rip. A baby tries on the body and finds that it is unwearable. *No, this will not do. My light will leak.* A new one must be started from scratch. And so, tenderly, tranquilly, it severs the cord and floats away. Or the body is fine, but the baby is never meant to be a baby: it is a teacher. Or it may be the mother who cuts the cord to release the baby back to the stars and back to the lake, where it rests on the shores, peaceful and free. In this case also, the baby is often a teacher.

The child takes the woman deeper into her eyes, and the woman sees that the child is no child; she is ancient, older than the woman, older than fire. One warm summer night, she saw the woman scream, the house burn down, and the husband rise like a plume of smoke, and she lowered herself along the cord to see what the commotion was about. She and the husband met briefly in the air, he on his way up, she on her way down.

"Love," he cried, as he swept around and through his daughter.

"Love," she agreed, rushing inside him.

He gazed upon his wife, sobbing in the grass. "Compassion," he said, and it was not a description but a direction. The child felt the word, its down-feather fabric, and knew what she had to do. She clenched the cord until it withered and returned herself to the sky, to guide the woman from above rather than within. Compassion, to cease being her child? No, compassion to become her North Star.

"Love," the child says now to the woman. Her voice is insistent, almost pleading. *Don't you see?*

As the child holds the woman in her arms, the woman holds the child in her arms. They are one; they have never been otherwise. The woman had herself once stood on the banks of time, listening for two voices to harmonize. The pieces of her body were then quilted together and a little egg sewn into the cloth. Inside that egg was her child, some intrinsic form or fragment of her. To grieve something that has not—that cannot—ever be separated from her: it is nonsense. Mother and child have never been apart. Child has always been in mother, part of mother, even when mother is child. Mother has held child forever. And death is powerless, it is meaningless, against forever.

The woman yawns, exhausted from dying, from being born. She fights sleep, not wanting to miss a moment of her child. She has lost too many already. She cannot risk waking up to discover that the most heavenly of all the daughter universes has disappeared before her eyes.

The child places her hands on the woman's heart and soothes its skittish beat. "Love," she sings, and it is the only lyric in her song.

The woman reaches for the word, brings it to her cheek, buries her face in its warmth. *Memorize how this feels,* she commands herself. *Arrange this fabric into notes. Touch it, and let it touch us. Teach the others this most beautiful of all the music lessons: that death is a lullaby.*

There are no lessons though, not anymore. There is nothing to be memorized. All that exists is her child, with whom she has an eternity to spend. And once you realize that you have eternity, you no longer need memory, its crude substitute.

The thought relaxes her. "Love," she mumbles as she drifts off, drowsy with bliss, lost in the clouds of her child's voice. She falls into a slumber so deep that she does not even stir when the nurses come to lift her from her daughter and carry her away.

‽

8va

*T*he woman emerges from a wormhole of unconsciousness. The warmth recedes. The love does too. In their place is an immense abyss, which enters and overtakes her field of vision, filling it completely. It is as black as the night sky in which she swam, though, unlike the sky, it quivers with a nervous energy. The energy fixates on her, invites her inside, swallows her whole. She tries to look away. It follows her. It will not let go of her. She slowly moves her head and, with enough distance, discovers that she is staring into the black hole of the mare's eye, which stares back at her, unblinking.

The mare. The thought brings her a brief joy, and then the joy turns to something else, something with teeth. *The mare, but not my daughter.*

It is comfortable to slide back inside one's old body, in the same way that it is comfortable to sink into well-worn bedsheets. But nothing could ever be as comfortable or as soft as her daughter's arms.

The woman's blurry surroundings begin to take form. One becomes a table, on which *Music Lessons* sits. Another is the harp resting on the floor. On both sides are rows and rows of hospital beds, one of which contains her. She does not know exactly where she is. All that matters is where she is not. This place has dissonance. It has coldness. It has that thing shooting through her, shocking her. What is that thing? Oh yes, she remembers now. It is pain.

The pain of a child slipping through her grasping fingers, over and over again.

The pain of more endless, empty days.

She inspects her ankle. Instead of bite marks, she finds two perfectly parallel freckles, which will remain with her for the rest of her life. That very word—*life*—is another puncture wound, one deeper and rawer. If she must resume her life, why not her daughter and her husband? Why is she tethered to this weighty body when they are allowed to fly free? Even her prayers cannot ascend. Their wings have been broken. They just fall and lie crumpled at her feet.

A thousand times she has let go of grief, and it has returned to her a thousand more. She had not known that, like the universe, it could clone itself. That loss is a hall of mirrors, that its face would appear no matter where she turned. Now that she has held her child, any desire she might have had to go on living without her is gone. The antlike being has chosen to stay behind in the sea of stars, enraptured by that which it had resisted for so long. She yearns to join it, to go back to wherever she was. Being taken from there feels like a curse, a cruelty.

To her friend, though, it is pure relief. The days of a horse pass differently from those of a human; they gallop. The mare does not know how long it has spent waiting by her side, watching for any movement, forsaking its own. For each moment her eyes stayed closed, it kept its own open. Now, seeing her rise, it can rest. It lays its head, heavy with the sleeps that it has sacrificed, upon her chest. Finally its dreams are allowed to run loose and wild, reined in only by the gates of its eyelashes.

. . .

A breeze drifts by the bed, tousles the mare's mane, blows the curtains in and out. *What now, what now,* it whispers.

The woman glances around, finds only a shadow of the wind. "You brought me back from the dead," she says to no one, to anyone. "How?" The next question is even more important and mysterious: "Why?"

The answer to both is the same. The breeze sweeps past her book and ruffles its pages. It glides between the strings of the harp, creating a tune which the woman has never before heard yet which feels as familiar to her, as deeply a part of her, as a cradlesong from her childhood.

Then it brushes past the woman's ears and opens them. Instantly, she can hear everything: the hum of the vibrating walls, beds, people; the high-pitched chatter of the cells inside her; the harmony of the mare's sighs, of its liquid eyes.

"What? What is it?" she asks, but the breeze has already spoken, and it slips away.

.   .   .

Her body has been restored. The mare witnessed the effort this took, how the nurses stood over her and chanted in unison above her ankle. How they dove into the waters of time to stop the snake from tearing into her skin. How their unearthly voices charmed it with song and convinced it not to strike, knowing that where there is music, there can be no bite. How the hands that took her from her daughter were the same ones that plunged into her chest and reset the rhythm of her heart.

The heart, the heart—that is where the real work begins.

She has no idea how to revive this one part of her that still lies dead. Death is no longer a question once you have been through it, once you have been born on the other side of it. The question becomes, rather, life. Specifically: If all you want is to return to the place where your dead child is, then what makes you live? How do you go about creating a life in which you have no interest in participating?

The woman looks around, as though the walls held the answers. They reveal nothing. Her eyes fall in frustration and catch sight of *Music Lessons*, lying open to the page bookmarked by the breeze.

SONG OF HEALING

She lifts the harp from the floor. This effort alone is an exertion—dying is demanding on the body, it asks everything of it—yet there is something about music that eases pain even as it causes it. She tries the piece in front of her. The melody passes from the paper to her fingers, and when it reaches her ears she does not believe them. It is the same song composed by the wind as it blew between the strings.

The white light spins around her hands. And they are no longer only her hands. Her daughter's are wrapped around them. This is the secret of great musicians: they do not play alone.

A man lies in the bed next to her, listening to the sound of four hands acting as two, of two souls acting as one. His own longs to join them, though his motionless body cannot comply. So the notes come to him. They touch him. They fill him until he is made of music, and he finds that he can move, because the music moves him.

As she watches this, something numb inside the woman also begins to awaken. She gives the paralyzed man a dance. He gives the paralyzed woman a purpose. The song of healing is for them both. *It's a miracle*, she thinks, looking at him, but a miracle is simply love at its most audible.

She rifles through the book, searching for more. SONG OF
WEDDING WILDFLOWERS. The notes are dormant, buried somewhere deep inside her, yet as she plays them they break into
bloom. They climb the trellis of the musical staff and transform into lotuses—wildflowers live for seasons, lotuses for
centuries. PSALM, which means "plucking of the harp strings."
Every sound she makes is sacred. SONG OF A LITTLE BIRD ("Why
oh why so blue? Because it ate a blue fruit"). And then, for the
little bird that has grown: SONG OF A PHOENIX, BORN FROM THE
ASHES OF FIRE.

The pieces that had once seemed impossible now unfold
effortlessly beneath her fingers. The skills and the drills. The
lessons, the lifetimes.

The dance of ecstasy taking place before her eyes.

She has come back to master them all.

· · ·

Each night the woman sits under the planets and listens to
their slow, arcane music. She searches the skies for her husband
and finds him blazing past the clouds, igniting the darkness, a
man turned meteor. Her ears unlocked, she hears him everywhere. "Sing me a love song," he once asked of her, yet now it
is he who serenades her, and in a hundred voices: the trembling
of aspens, a katydid choir, the murmur of April rain. She tran-
scribes the sounds in the margins of *Music Lessons.* With starlight

as her reading lamp, she loses herself in the book's pages, in the secrets of its songs.

Each morning she walks the wards of the field hospital with her harp, ministering to the sick and ailing, to those not as easily extricated from death as she. And there are always more and more people streaming in who need her help: people that groan and people that bleed and people with souls that refuse to budge or that remain connected by only the slightest string. To tend to all of them would take years, though the woman has plenty of those to spare. Her days, and soon her repertoire, become ceaseless.

Some will die, for to heal is not necessarily the same as to cure. With fright they watch her approach, expecting a dirge yet hearing a lullaby. This, she thinks, must be another reason why the nurses saved her and why she had to return: to sing of death's sweetness, to tuck its blanket of comfort around the patients' shoulders. After all, how many times had death laid its music at her feet? Why else would it have spared the musician, except to share its sound?

An elderly man arrives, leaning his limbs on a wooden stick, and slowly disassembles himself bone by bone as he climbs into a bed. The woman stands beside his gnarled legs and helps smooth out his body so that it is supine. As her hands move over him, they unfasten his joints, gaining entry to the suffering stored within. The motion she makes reminds her of something that she cannot quite place. It takes her a moment to recognize it as the same technique the wartime doctor used on her patients. A recollection of a future already experienced—an inverse *déjà vu*.

The man curls up like a fetus, resembling an ancient baby. For him she plays SONG OF LOVE. All music derives from it. It is older than the song of grief that she had sung that long-ago day in the forest, for grief can only occur if love precedes it. There is a single lyric, just as her daughter has taught her.

The piece does not come to an end; a song of love knows no limits. But the man has heard what he needs to hear. He hops off the bed, walks away, leaves the stick behind.

• • •

An infant's skin is burned and inflamed. The woman understands her distress, for she too has been scarred by fire. She applies a poultice of strings and nursery rhymes to the sore flesh. The skin becomes calm. The infant's eyes, mouth, and breath form a triad of surprise. The sight of it causes the woman to laugh with joy.

Laughter. It has been so long since the mare heard her make this noise. The melody of the sound soothes its injured leg, and the discomfort that has accompanied its every step now disappears. Elated, it prances around the infant's bed. To walk again is freedom, to laugh again even more so.

The woman's heart soars to see her friend rid of its pointless pain. The mare looks at the woman, feels the same.

. . .

The woman encounters a body that has almost no soul left inside it. The body is so old and threadbare that the soul spends most of its time on the outside, living between the stars rather than under them. Neither body nor soul will mind what the woman is about to do.

She musters her strength, thrusts her white-light hands into the abdomen, and extracts the DNA. The strands coil around her fingers, and she watches in amazement as the double helix unfurls and lies flat in her palm. Once it is two-dimensional, its shape becomes unmistakable: it is a musical staff. Each nucleotide is a note arranged on a line, each base pair an interval. People, the woman realizes, are nothing more than—no, nothing less than—a symphony.

In one hand she holds the molecules, in the other she holds her harp. And then she combines them and plays the ballad of the body. The opening notes are silvery and birdlike, dipping into and out of common time. The tempo increases. The treble of boyhood deepens into bass. Here comes the jazz of a young man's city nights, the blues of an old man waking too early, too alone. Broken chords and promises and bones. A sudden pause in the piece and the sound does not flow; a sudden pause of the heart and the blood does not flow. The brain turns to silence. The soul turns to the stars.

Every musician knows how to improvise. The woman studies the genes and, after some thought, chooses a new mode. She modulates the key, phrases things a different way. Now the music belongs not to the man in the bed but to a falcon in an egg. She hears the determined eighth notes as it pecks its way out, the falsetto of its flight, the chord progression from small, shelled being into ruler of the skies.

Four notes, she thinks, *to build every body, to compose every opus.*

She rearranges the notation, returning it to the human. She removes entire measures and then, her fingers on the strings, takes it from the top. The very old body transforms into a very young one. It lengthens and silkens, becomes as smooth as her song. The more she plays, the more it grows younger, then smaller, until it is that of a newborn taking its first breath, and the soul leaves the stars and swoops back into the body to be that breath, and its life, like its song, begins again.

. . .

She and the mare travel from patient to patient. The mare presses its warm muzzle against muscles that have forgotten how to move. The woman matches the pulse of patient and song. She regulates vital rhythms, attends to any erratic syncopation. Her steady hands and harp keep the beat for those who cannot. Her tones are a tuning fork with which their cells resonate. And on the occasions when their spirits leave to swim inside a glimmering expanse of sky, she accompanies them with her music, with her memories of that floating freedom, and sings them a happy birthday.

One day, a nurse stops to observe her. At the end of the session, she pats the woman's shoulder, pleased.

"I understand now," the woman says to her. "I'm preparing for the work I'll do in another life as a doctor."

"No," the nurse replies. "This is preparation for your work as a musician."

The nurse's warm touch melts the woman; her fears seep out. "I know that I can stay here and spend the rest of my days caring for those in pain, just as you do. But is this meant to be my way—is this meant to be my life? Sleeping alone under the stars, dreaming dreams that disappear, playing someone else's music instead of making my own? I worry that I've not found my footing, that I never will."

"Why worry? The notes you play don't worry about what will come next; they just let themselves ring out. They trust that the musician knows how the song is supposed to sound."

The fears, however, keep flowing. "I worry that I'll only be able to heal the others, and not myself."

"Healing the others," says the nurse, "is another name for healing yourself."

. . .

An opera singer and a glass resonate at different frequencies. The singer raises her voice; she raises her volume. She changes her wavelength, hits the highest note she can. Now she and the glass sing the same song. The glass absorbs her energy, is shattered by the intensity. It can no longer bear to be what it was—solid, physical, vibrating by its lonesome. It bursts with excitement into a new state of being.

If a soul, like a singer, decided to raise its vibration and its volume, to grow in amplitude, to elevate itself until it resonated at the frequency of love, who in its presence could ever stay the same? Would they not be lifted to its level? And could the world contain such magnificence, or might it shatter with the energy and break open into something new?

· · ·

PLAY THE A ABOVE MIDDLE C.

The woman does.

THIS IS CALLED CONCERT A. IT IS THE STANDARD FOR TUNING INSTRUMENTS. IT HAS A FREQUENCY OF 440 HZ. NOW PLAY IT AN OCTAVE HIGHER.

Her fingers climb seven strings and pluck the note.

DESCRIBE THE DIFFERENCE YOU HEAR IN THE NOTES.

I don't hear any.

THIS PHENOMENON IS CALLED OCTAVE EQUIVALENCE. THE NOTES SOUND THE SAME, BUT THE LATTER RESONATES AT 880 HZ, DOUBLE THE FREQUENCY OF THE FORMER. THEY ARE ONE NOTE, VIBRATING AT DIFFERENT LEVELS. NAME THAT NOTE.

The note is A.

TRY AGAIN.

The note is love.

Every note is love.

It can be played in the octave of romantic love, in the octave of familial love, or in the highest octave, universal love, which often lies beyond the perception of the human ear.

To become enamored with another person, to sing together so sweetly that you leave the world behind, to see the eyes of God looking out through the eyes of a man: the woman understands that some beings take on a body for this reason alone. After all, is she not one of them? She and her husband have spent eons making music, dipping into time again and again to continue their duet.

But this is only one form of love.

Others take on life in order to create life, to bear the body of a child and the crosses of a parent; she knows this also, having attempted it herself. And this is no minor undertaking. One day the heart will evolve in size, will grow large enough to comfortably contain a mother's love. Until then, it may rupture with the pressure.

But this, too, is only one form.

A person may be infatuated with a mountain's contours, a riverbed's curves. With the paintbrush or prayer book in her hands. With the earnest stare of his dog, the depths of devotion in its gaze. The expression depends on the particular instrument; some will have a limited range, while others can span several octaves. This does not mean that one is inferior or superior to another. It simply means that they produce different sounds.

Eventually, the body is taken on to love the all as well as the you, and the life taken on to love not one person but every person. Not your child but every child. Not the lives connected to yours but all lives, because all lives are connected to yours. To serve every soul, whether it be played in the octave of maple leaf, of mare, of man, knowing that they are all made of music, that they are the same one note—that there is only one note, vibrating at varying rates—and that the note is ineffably, incomprehensibly beautiful.

WITH ENOUGH PRACTICE, THE DISTINCTION BECOMES CLEAR.

FORM A CHORD COMPRISED OF THE SAME NOTE IN THREE SEPARATE OCTAVES.

Using both hands, the woman strikes the notes at once—romantic love, familial love, and the love beyond that, which is a love beyond everything. Her patients have been listening, and they begin to sing along. The chorus of their compassion fills her with emotion, sends her frequency surging. She takes her fingers off the first two strings. Perhaps it is all right if those notes are missing, if they are silent. She can make the same sound with the third.

THE OCTAVE IS CALLED THE BASIC MIRACLE OF MUSIC.

When really it is the basic miracle of life.

THIS CONCLUDES THE LESSON.

• • •

CONGRATULATIONS.

YOU HAVE COME TO THE END OF THE BOOK.

YOUR STUDIES ARE NEARLY FINISHED.

YOUR MUSIC LESSONS ARE COMING TO A CLOSE.

BUT FIRST, THERE IS ONE FINAL PIECE YOU MUST LEARN.

ONCE YOU MASTER IT, YOU WILL HAVE COMPLETED YOUR ASSIGNMENT.

IT IS THE SONG THAT WILL GIVE YOUR LIFE ITS MEANING.

IT IS THE SONG FOR WHICH YOU HAVE BEEN SEARCHING ALL THIS TIME.

IT IS THE SONG OF YOUR SOUL.

KEEP READING.

YOU ARE ALMOST THERE.

THE ANSWER TO EVERYTHING IS ON THE NEXT PAGE.

THIS PAGE INTENTIONALLY LEFT BLANK

≀

Interlude

*A*s is every page after that.

The woman flips furiously through the rest of the book, through the empty pages that contain no instruction, no notation, neither song nor secret.

"Where is it?" she demands. The mare does not answer.

"Where is it?" she says again, but the mare cannot answer. Only the woman can.

All this time she has been traveling with no direction, running away instead of toward, and now direction appears before her and stands at command. She will find the author of *Music Lessons*, will tell this deranged Anonymous that a book once begun, like a marriage, like a life, cannot end in sudden silence. A sonata must have its coda. The swan must have its song. How can the creator of something so unbearably beautiful as music—and as man—not know this most basic rule?

The nurse and the patients tilt their heads and listen, for intention, like sound, carries through the air and grows amplified with energy. They gather around her. The sight of their concerned faces makes the woman stop short.

"How can I leave them?" she asks the nurse. "They need my help, my healing."

"Healing yourself," says the nurse, "is another name for healing the others."

One by one the patients shuffle past her and say good-bye, shaking her hand, humming a tune she has taught them, petting the mare's nose. Then the last in line walks away, and there is no one left to treat and nothing more to play. She has given them all the music she has. Now she must find the missing piece.

She must find the song of her soul.

She leads the mare away from the hospital and hops on its back. It sprints until its muscles gasp for air, and then sprints faster. The outside world is encased in snow and ice, though inside the woman is a fire—not one of death but of life. It lights her, it lights the mare beneath her and the ice beneath the mare. The mare is powered by its newly restored legs, by the euphoria of motion freed from confinement; the woman by something else, something internal, something unfamiliar.

Something like hope.

. . .

How do you find what you are looking for when you have no idea where to look for it?

Can movement that gets nowhere be considered movement at all?

The days run together, or perhaps it is simply one day, frozen in place. The cold is three-dimensional. It surrounds the mare and the woman and shadows their every step, an unshakable companion. They huddle together to keep warm, to keep the fire inside them from dying out. The smoke plumes they exhale are the only evidence that it still burns.

They ride on, pausing solely for the mare to drink the snow. The woman looks around while the mare fills itself with fallen clouds. In a nearby tree, an eagle dozes in its nest, its eyelids descending in increments. Silently, smoothly, the wind sneaks through its feathers, lifting them and lowering them, over and over. She watches, transfixed by the soundless rhythm of the earth breathing a bird in and out.

Above their heads, Orion stalks the stars for his prey. His migration is constant, his hunt endless. Night after night, instead of resting, he perseveres. In this way, he is like the woman. With each passing year, the pieces of him separate and shift. Eventually, he will be misshapen, unrecognizable. Then his hunt must become for himself, for the errant parts that will make him whole once more.

In this way, too, they are alike.

• • •

Their run slows to a walk, the walk to a crawl, the hope to dismay. The earth sheds it winter coat, too warm to wear it any longer. Blades of grass rise on its body like beads of sweat. Nature pops its head out from underground. The sun is meek at first, then overbearing. The crickets sing it to sleep. The mare and the woman keep moving.

One leaf keels over and dies, and the rest follow suit. The flowers turn to frost, the streams to ice, the bears to sleep. The moon weaves its web of months around them; the sun becomes snared in the trap, and the world calls this winter. The mare and the woman keep moving.

Snow and weeks crunch beneath their feet. The days press on the woman's face and create furrows. Gravity presses on her back and shortens her spine. Her skin grows as brittle and speckled as a quail's egg. There is so much walking yet no finding. This presses on the heart. And somehow, despite the force, the mare and the woman keep moving.

They come, at last, to a river covered in ice. It might support the weight of their bodies, but not of their disappointment. They could wait for it to thaw, although that too offers little opportunity to cross. The river is no gentle lake of time; there are rapids lying in wait below its surface, and hibernation will have made them hungry.

It is a dead end. They can go no farther. There is only backward, or so the woman thinks, not realizing that backward can also be forward.

She sinks to her knees in the snow and lowers her face into her hands. She should have stayed at the hospital. Her life had purpose there. So what if she never found its meaning, its completion? At least she wouldn't have to keep looking for it.

I've chosen the wrong path, she thinks. *Why is it always the wrong path?*

But impassable—and even impossible—is not the same as wrong.

. . .

The woman and the mare reverse direction. They walk anywhere, everywhere.

Spring closes in on winter; summer trails behind, hot on its heels. Far off in the shimmering haze, a movement catches the mare's attention. It is inconsequential, a cloud of dragonflies changing course in the air. But to the mare, having watched the woman die, every dragonfly is a flying dragon in disguise; all things have the potential to turn snake. It snorts and stares, vigilant in its anxiety. *I must contain this threat and anticipate the next, or else we may get hurt.*

The woman can see the situation from a higher perspective, a better vantage point. She knows that the dragonflies won't come any closer, and that they would pose no danger if they did. "Relax," she says, stroking the mare's mane, wishing to calm its needless fear. "You're perfectly safe. Everything is fine. Nothing will harm you."

At that moment, a rustle of the grasses, the same words in her own ear.

. . .

The days grow short. The woman grows weary.

To be by her side every step of the way: this is what her husband had promised her, both with body and without. But when there is no way, and the steps are incalculable—what then?

"Please," she begs him, "guide me. Instead of standing behind, walk in front. Lead me to the one who knows my song, my end."

She would give anything to see footprints, track marks, some sign of his that she could follow. Only the birches, shivering in the cold, make their presence known. They are worn down to skeletons, their bony branches revealing nests that were once homes, now husks.

She has watched it happen every year, the systematic approach of the starkest season. The leaves blush and swoon, the wind bites and stings, the birds fade away. Yet birdless days do not mean a birdless world; to disappear from sight is not to disappear from existence. They are simply in another place, a warmer one. And they always return in time.

It would be foolish to grieve the bird that has flown south; it would be criminal to grab hold of its legs and confine it to the earth. Then why, she must ask herself, does she insist that her husband walk with her? She cannot keep asking this of him, not anymore. It is her turn to take the lead.

Give him back to me, she had insisted once. *And now, I will give him back to you.*

She turns her face to the frozen sky. "Fly on home," she tells him, and with a whisper of wings he is gone, soaring higher and higher toward the light, until he is the light.

. . .

The woman stops walking and indicates the mare should do the same. She takes out her harp. She will cover ground in a different way, set forth with her fingers instead of footsteps, spirit instead of body. Music allows this—in fact, demands it.

She opens to the first page of *Music Lessons* and begins to play her book and her life from start to finish, until she comes to those blank pages that sent her hunting for the song that would fill them. The harp is an instrument of translation as well as of music. It tells the story of her pain in another voice, in the language of the strings, where the word for *sorrow* is the same as the one for *beauty.*

A sob rises above the melodies, as if trying to harmonize with them. The mare's eyes are dry, and horses weep with their tails, not their tears. It must be coming from somewhere else. It must be coming from her.

Her intention had been to summon an author. Instead, she casts out a demon. All her anger and all her failure come rolling out in chords, in a downward-spiraling glissando. Defeat, despair: they are made of lead—gray, dense, dangerous—but the music lends them feathers. As they make their way outside her and away from her, the woman, freed from their weight, feels as if she too might rise into the air. Sound is strong enough to do this. It is nearly as powerful as love and often indistinguishable from it, for much of love is sound and sound love: a cat's purr, a mother's coo, a bride's beating heart. And then there is the most powerful sound of all.

She puts down her harp, holds the book in both hands, and, one last time, studies its empty pages for an answer. But there is no answer, and that is the answer. Music is the sound that is sculpted from silence, and so to find the music, one must first find the silence. It is time to be quiet. It is time to rest. It is time to call off the search. She will never find what she is looking for. And this is when she finally finds what she is looking for, because you can only find yourself when you stop moving and become still.

{

Crescendo

"*H*ere you are," her higher self says. "What took you so long?"

The woman stands face-to-face with her own face. All those years, all those miles, in search of the one thing that had been with her everywhere she went? She is suddenly tired, feeling that she has spent her life walking in circles. As though progress could only be linear; as though a circle were an error, and not a revolution.

"The ice—the snow—the grief—they take a long time to plow through."

"If you say so."

Astounded and delighted, the mare rushes over to its new old friend for a nuzzle. The woman, breathless with exhaustion, with need, thrusts *Music Lessons* into the higher self's hands, shows her the empty pages of which she is already well aware. It was she who wrote it, after all; she who, a thief in reverse, slipped into the barn one night and hid it in the hay for the woman to find and use as a guide. That is what higher selves do. They steal into unlit places, light them on fire, leave the ashes behind as a trail.

"What is the song that gives my life its meaning, the song of my soul? How does it go?" the woman asks.

"You tell me."

"I must know the ending of the book."

"Then write it."

That is the task of the author, not the reader! The woman falls silent again, but her silence is loud with frustration.

"You are the writer of your story. You are the creator of your song." The higher self's eyes are recognizable to the woman as her own, though they are also foreign—softer, deeper. "You are a composer, and life is your greatest work of art."

• • •

"Follow me," says the higher self, striding across the slippery fields. The woman rushes to keep up with her.

They walk, the mare trotting at their side, until they reach the frozen river. "It's too risky," the woman protests. The higher self calmly takes hold of the mare's mane and the woman's hand, and together they cross with ease. The ice does not crack or collapse. There can be no danger when your higher self is carrying you. In her arms, you weigh nothing.

On the other side of the river, hidden behind the birches, is a cabin where the higher self has been waiting, patiently, for the woman to join her. The mare stays outside to race the falling flurries. The others enter. The higher self gestures for the woman to sit at the wooden desk in the center of the room, then places *Music Lessons* in front of her. "Go on," she says, resting her hand on the woman's back. "Finish it."

The woman takes a pen from a drawer and puts it to paper. Nothing comes out. Her mind is too clogged for any sound to flow from its nib.

She lifts her eyes from the pages. "How do I compose the music?"

The higher self regards her, amused. Sometimes no one can surprise you more than yourself. "You've been doing it all this time."

"But I didn't know that I was."

That is the difference. To know changes everything.

"Does your husband ever visit you in dreams?" the higher self asks, knowing the answer already, having dreamed the dreams herself.

"He used to," the woman replies. "I wish he still would."

"Then make it happen."

"I can't just 'make it happen.' Dreams are not in one's control." Neither is life, she thinks: a husband who died as a gift, a daughter as a favor; the snake that stopped her heart, the nurses that stopped her death. "Nothing is."

"Everything is. That's what makes this such fun."

The woman is aware that the dream world is surreal, its boundaries fluid. She is not yet aware that the waking world is too. The difference is that the dreamer accepts this fact while the waker resists it. One loosens her grip on space, on time, on the conscience, on the body; the other hangs on for dear life. One conforms to the logic of the place in which she finds herself; the other imposes her will on it, not realizing that to renounce control is to gain it. One finds her wishes fulfilled; the other, dissolved.

"When you are asleep, and you know that you are asleep," the higher self says, "you are lucid. *Lucid* means 'seeing clearly': not only that you are dreaming, but that there is nothing to restrict you apart from your own mind. Do you wish to fly? Just throw yourself into the arms of the sky and let the wind hold you. Do you wish to talk with me? To read what's waiting to be written in your book? To learn the language of the moon, to speak its secrets to your husband, to spend each night beside him?"

"Yes," the woman breathes.

"All that is stopping you," says the higher self, "is you."

.   .   .

Here you are, my little bird.
You're here? I thought you'd left.
That old song and dance?
I suppose it's time for a new one.

Since the night of the fire, how many times have I come to you in dreams?

Many.

When you woke, how many times did you find me lying next to you?

None.

Every time I've been with you, it's been a dream.

Must you twist the knife?

And I am with you now.

Which means that I am dreaming.

Yes.

Which means that I am aware I am dreaming.

Yes.

Which means that I can do anything.

So, what would you like to do?

. . .

The woman could not lose her husband if she tried. She released him, and he came back. She searched her dreams and found him inside them. She played her songs and found him inside them. Death had not claimed him; it had multiplied him.

"What would you like to do?" he asks her, night after night. It is as if he offers her the universe, yet instead of taking it she transcends it. Freedom is one thing; freedom with power, another entirely. The possibilities are delicious, electric. It is her world to create—one with walls made of rubber instead of steel, where families grow old instead of bleed out, where she is not a victim but a god.

"Open your eyes," she can hear the higher self say. The woman does not obey. When her surroundings are finally as she desires them, why would she ever leave?

The higher self waits, knowing that there is no escaping yourself. Knowing that life is but a dream, and just as dreams melt and morph, so does life. A lotus in a pond blooms into a schoolgirl on a train. The dorsal fin of a sailfish flattens into the mane of a mare. Fear, loss, grief: this is the material from which nightmares are made, but nightmares can occur only in one whose eyes are closed. To be lucid is not to be aware that you are dreaming while you are asleep. It is to be aware of it while you are awake.

The higher self cannot be the one to wake the woman, anyhow. The woman must do it; otherwise, she will never become the higher self. And so she simply lies down next to the woman, cradles her in her arms, and starts to sing: "Little bird, blue bird, why oh why so blue?"

"Because it ate a blue fruit," the woman responds from somewhere inside her sleep, consciousness being a fence under which music can crawl.

So, too, can a higher self, and she sneaks into that walled-off place with a whisper.

"Little bird," she says, "what will compel you to peck your way out of your shell? If you stay inside too long, you'll suffocate. When will you see that the very thing which protects you is the very thing which confines you, and crack it wide open?"

After some time the woman stirs, and the visions that have been her unequivocal reality disintegrate. She tries to hold on to them, but they flee. Perhaps the higher self is right, she thinks, and the waking world is indeed like the dreaming one. After all, hers has been no less illogical or impermanent: the everyday giving way to the unfamiliar; people vanishing into the air, or materializing from it; all that chasing, flying, dying. She had declared herself to be at its mercy, never recognizing that it was at hers, that a life is indeed made of clay and not stone. What if she were to put her hands to it, to mold it into some new shape? To smooth out its painful contours, to view it as unformed rather than deformed? Or to set it aside and start over on a completely different piece? She imagines running her fingers along the clay as she does with her harp, coaxing something beautiful from something gray. The white light appears. The hands of the higher self cover her own. They will work together.

The woman has just begun her lucid dreams. Now she begins her lucid life.

. . .

The higher self unlocks a door, and the woman passes through it.

As the woman steps into the room, she notices an enormous telephone switchboard spanning its length. The cables connect not lines but life. Her decisions to their consequences. One footstep to the next. To her eyes it is a hopeless snarl of cords and wires, incapable of being untangled.

The higher self waits to the side. "Stand farther back," she suggests.

The woman does, and the distance brings order into being. One end of a cord is plugged into a jack labeled FIRE. Its other end hangs loose. She scans the empty jacks. GIFT. LESSON. GUILT. She need not keep looking; she knows where FIRE fits. It is a well-worn groove. She plugs the loose end of the cord into GUILT. The action is automatic, comforting.

The higher self sees that this is a bad connection, one that creates static. She lights up other options, as higher selves do.

FORGIVENESS and ACCEPTANCE blink with promise. To plug the cord into either of them would take just a moment, a motion. Yet somehow the effort required to cross those few inches of space, to close that circuit, is tremendous. The woman's hand is able to do it. Her mind is not.

The higher self does not understand her reluctance. "What's the worst that can happen?"

The woman's voice is small. "It might not fit."

"Then you keep trying until it does."

She is hardly able to look as she tests both of them out, though the cord slips into those sockets as easily as it did into GUILT. There is no resistance from the cord, from the jack, from the higher self—only from her.

The switchboard regenerates, new patterns forming and new potentials arising, for what ensues from guilt and innocence, from fault and forgiveness, are not the same. Emboldened, she slides one end of the cord out of ACCEPTANCE and attempts to yank the other end free from FIRE. It will not budge; she will not stop. The higher self must finally intervene, telling her, "It was not your decision to make."

GRIEF has its own circuit. What would have occurred had the woman chosen to defy the antlike being and remain inside her charred house forever, a slowly dying ember of a person? She unplugs the cord from Go and inserts it into STAY. The switchboard becomes as bare as that life would have been. No connections. No light.

Hers might have been an impossible path—but not the wrong one.

IF ONLY connects to VERSE or to REFRAIN.

SONG to MOURNING DOVE or to STARLING.

WARRIOR to WOMAN, WOMAN to WARRIOR.

ACORN to OAK.

The board is solved, the snarl silenced. A signal lamp flicks on. Someone is calling.

The woman is unsure what to do next. "How do I make the connection?"

"Just step back."

Now she can plainly see how the lines of communication must be joined, and when she plugs in the wire, the channel is crisp and clear. "Who's there?" she asks.

"Me," says the higher self.

•   •   •

"Surely, life cannot be so readily changed," the woman argues. Surely it is less permutation than prison. A husband caged inside his attic, his wife inside her grief, no risk of flight because she clips her own wings. A person incarcerated for a crime he did not commit, or in a body he did not deserve. The jail's cells, the body's cells: their walls are solid, inescapable.

When this happens, the one end of the cable cannot be removed. It is locked in place. The other end cannot be left dangling, though. It must be plugged in somewhere. She considers the connections. It fits into the jack for BITTERNESS, for ANGER—oh, how well it fits there.

"Step back," the higher self says.

The woman steps back and sees a new space open up, a new possibility. The mind can transcend the thoughts and the emotions, can even transcend the jail. A body may be forced into fetters, but a soul cannot. Once this is understood, the sentence is completed.

"Step back."

The switchboard is one of many in a never-ending row. One belongs to the prisoner, another to the warden, to the victim, to the committer of the crime. One to the virus and one to the host, to the patient, the doctor, the disease. Their cords are entwined, inseparable, crossing over and over.

"Step back."

Victim and villain, prisoner and warden, judge and juror: they are all the same person.

"Step back."

To sacrifice one lifetime in captivity—to surrender physical freedom for the freedom of the consciousness—is to leapfrog over many more. It is not imprisonment but the opposite.

The cable comes loose in her hands.

. . .

It is the winter of the woman's life, and the snow is falling fast. It erases the fields and hills, buries her tracks, muffles her pains. Everything is white: the mare's tattered bones, the sky, those final pages that wait to be filled. The higher self will help her do this. They share the same past, the same pen, although one is musician and the other is maestro. And it is never too late to begin writing one's music. There is no getting older— only higher.

The woman sits on a snowbank, *Music Lessons* in her lap. She rereads a passage that has confounded her since she first came across it, this time aloud so the higher self can hear.

CRESCENDO

MUSIC GRADUALLY BUILDS TOWARD A CLIMAX AND DIES. MANY CONSIDER THIS THE END OF THE PIECE. IT IS MERELY THE BEGINNING.

"Ah, yes, the crescendo," the higher self says. "To fully understand the concept, you must first understand the most important moment of your life. Would you like to see what it is?"

The woman's breath freezes inside her. The climax of the music is what every composer strives for, what every listener longs for. It must be the answer to her empty pages—the answer to her.

On the icy ground, images appear, a scene forms. The mare leans down for a closer look. The woman watches too, expecting wedding-day wildflowers, smoke and cinders, snakebite. Instead, she sees herself as a toddler. The young girl is running around the yard, nearly dancing, for at that age all movement is a dance. She spots something still and dark in the grass and crouches down to inspect it. It is a winter wren, immobile except for its frightened eyes, its wild heart. The girl is astonished to find such treasure dropped from the skies. She cups her hands around its body. Her fingers are warm, her touch as soft as its feathers. "Don't worry. You'll fly again," she tells it, mistaking hope for truth, in the way children do. The girl and the wren are both so tiny, sitting there in the grass, but nothing is little about the love that passes between them.

The scene fades; ice becomes ice again. The higher self claps with glee, though the woman's mind is as blank as the snow surrounding her.

"That's all?" she says.

"That's all?" the higher self repeats. "That's *everything*."

. . .

A crescendo is swelling strings and crashing drums, not broken birds! Of everything the woman has ever done, this act was the most important—but what could be less so? She hadn't even formed a memory around it. She turns to the higher self, a question in her eyes.

The higher self is surprised to have to explain unconditional love. To love a tiny creature, to love all humankind, there is no difference. Love is love; the object is not the subject. And nothing is louder or more powerful. *"Crescendo* means 'growing.' What do you think you were doing for that bird's soul? And for your own?"

The little wren was no bigger than her child must have been, and that love had defied size. The woman knows how it felt to be placed in the hands of her daughter. Had the wren felt the same way in hers? Is life nothing more than a series of being mother to all that falls in one's hands? How strangely she has behaved, spending each day birthing and raising and nurturing everything around her—her patients, her mare, her music, herself—while crying that she is childless.

From beneath the snow comes activity; a shiver of feathers and the frost falls off, revealing the wren. Of course it is healthy and whole. It never was otherwise. Its wounds were only bone deep, its death only body deep. The wren was not really a wren, either. It was a living, breathing opportunity for compassion, which even at her young age the girl knew to cup in careful hands, to keep warm, to keep alive. This is what we all are: chances for each other to practice kindness, disguised as people.

The wren darts back and forth, more blur than bird, and comes to rest on the mare's back. Its feathers molt away. Its beak recedes. Where there was wren there is now light, growing ever larger and stronger until it eclipses the ice, the woman's eyes, the heavens. The higher self gestures downward, and the light, following her signal, compresses itself back into that miniature breast, a being greater than the sun tamped down into a body the size of a matchbox.

"Do not confuse the container," says the higher self, "with what it contains."

. . .

"A crescendo is an increase in power," she continues.

The woman believes she has already grasped the subject of power. She knows how to create worlds, how to control them. But this is power's manifestation, not its meaning.

"To become louder, to become quieter, to discover the strength in the softness: these are means of expression in music, and they are what move the listener. Beauty is born from the dynamics," says the higher self. "Power has its own dynamics, and it too can be played both *forte* and *pianissimo possibile,* as soft as possible."

"Soft power?" The woman chuckles.

"Yes, like the butterfly. No one expects it to be a firecracker. It wouldn't be a butterfly if it were, and it would devastate the flowers upon which it lands. Nevertheless, the power inherent inside it—to accept the dark days, knowing that they are when transformation occurs; to honor the time it takes for one's wings to dry; to slough off the weight of its past and fly, when all its life it has known only to crawl—is far more explosive than any firecracker. Soft can be so much stronger than hard."

"I know the power of my loss," the woman says, "and the strength. It ground my heart to gravel. It flattened my years. But the power of my life? I've lived in a small way, doing small things of which no one will ever know. There is nothing meaningful about it."

"Did you not see the wren, whose spirit is no smaller than the universe that contains it? No impulse of love is smaller than another. Had you never opened your heart to your loved ones or touched a single patient with your music, had you done nothing else with your time on earth but shown compassion to that one wren, it would still have been a triumph."

The woman shakes her head. An entire existence for a bird?

The higher self shakes her own head. No. An entire existence for a kindness.

"Decade upon decade of struggle, of survival, of eating and sleeping and bleeding and needing, of fire and ice and pain, all that pain—all that *life*—it can't possibly be worth it just for that," the woman says.

"It is not worth it. It *is* it."

"And on those days when being alive is too heavy a burden, let alone being kind?" She hesitates, though who can she admit this to, if not herself? Or is that, in fact, the hardest person to whom to confess it? "And on those days when your soul feels long dead, and you wish the same for your body?"

"There are billions of doors on your planet. Hold one open for someone. You don't have to compose the song that solves all suffering. One note is enough."

Kindness is the ultimate power, for everything kind is powerful. It is the greatest means of expression, a life played at its loudest. It may appear as a grace note, inessential, ephemeral—a flitting wren, a hand on a door—yet even if it seems trivial in size, even if it fades immediately from both melody and memory, it is the crescendo of the song and the soul.

Step back, the woman tells herself—or is it the higher self saying this? What is the difference anymore?

There is no wren. There is no door. There is no note. There is only easing the suffering of a fellow living creature. There is only adding more love to a world that once held less. What a beautiful basis for a person. What a resounding success of a life.

And what power!

. . .

"A crescendo is an increase in volume," the higher self says.

In the snow, another scene, another dimension. People standing on a busy sidewalk, waiting to cross the street, turning cold as a cloud empties its contents onto their shoulders. One holds an umbrella over her head. A businessman hails a taxi and climbs inside. Behind him are two little children and their grandfather, who checks his watch again and again. A car tries to merge into the traffic ahead of the taxi. *Will you let me in?* The taxi driver honks his horn no. A candy wrapper skitters along the ground, chased by the wind. Somebody's left a shopping cart outside. A mother tries to wheel her baby's stroller to the corner, slowly shifting it from curb to pavement. A beggar sits and watches her as he jingles his cup of coins. A pigeon lands at his side, scanning the cup for a scrap of food. A little girl nibbles on her hot dog and laughs at the funny way the pigeon bobs its head.

"What do you hear?" asks the higher self.

"Not much," the woman says.

"Turn up the volume, then."

The sidewalk, the people, the wind, the rain. The one with the umbrella holds it high over her head so that it will shield the others. The businessman hails a taxi and notices the grandfather behind him checking his watch. He must be in a rush. The businessman motions for the family to take his place. A car wants to pull in front of the taxi. The taxi driver waves his hand. *Go ahead.* The driver of the car waves her hand too, in gratitude. The wrapper is picked up and placed in the trash, the shopping cart brought back to the store. The mother wheels the stroller to the curb. The beggar rushes over and lifts the bottom of the stroller so that they can lower it onto the street. The one with the umbrella sees this and smiles. She places a bill in the beggar's cup. It is not much, but it is something. He says, "Bless you," and she looks in his eyes, and now two are blessed where once were none. The pigeon lands by the man's side and finds nothing to eat in his cup. The little girl laughs, tears off a piece of bun, and tosses it to the bird.

"Louder," the higher self says.

People, rain. The one with the umbrella holds it high over her head to shield the others, to let them know that she loves them. The businessman hails a taxi and notices the grandfather behind him checking his watch. "I love you," he says, motioning for the family to take his place. A car wants to pull in front of the taxi. The taxi driver waves the other driver in, love in another language. Someone places the wrapper in the trash, because the earth is loved; someone brings the shopping cart back to the store, because the shopkeeper is loved. The mother pushes the stroller. The beggar lifts the wheels. Together they place it on the street as the beggar says to her, "I love you and your child." The one with the umbrella sees this, smiles. She walks over and places a bill in his cup. It is not much, but it is love. He tells her he loves her, and to look in his eyes is to tell him the same. The pigeon lands by his side, looking for a morsel of love. The little girl tears off a piece of bun and tosses it to the bird, and her laughter, like all laughter, is love. It may be the most important moment in her entire life. Or it may be just the start.

The woman does not need to step back or turn up the sound. She can hear it clearly now: the music behind the movements, the harmony behind the discord. The song that solves all suffering— it is no mere song. It is a symphony. As she stumbled through her forest of grief and ice, she'd covered her ears, wished herself

dead, willed herself deaf. But the music had never stopped playing. She had just stopped listening.

"A crescendo is an increase in love," she realizes.

The higher self nods. "What better way for us to grow?"

}

Composition

All this time, the woman has been focused on how the music ends. It is the wrong question; the music does not end. The question is: How does it begin?

"It started long before this body," the higher self says. "And so, to hear it, you must go beyond the body."

"By dying?"

"That is one way to leave the body behind, but it is not the only one."

· · ·

The woman lies on her back, nestled in the snow. She catches her breath, unlocks her rib cage, and sets it free. She concentrates her attention on each limb, each muscle, each organ that belongs to her. One by one, she lets them go. Her body erases itself. She loses its contours. A force pushes her down into the earth. From the deepest place inside her comes a memory, a knowing: *This is how it felt to be lotus.* And with the roots of her outer self fixed firmly in place, her inner one is free to rise like a tendril toward the sun.

Once in the air, she observes herself on the ground, just as she had done when she died. This time she can see evidence of life: fluttering lids, a shiver up the spine. This time the mare is untroubled by her absence. It sleeps beside her in the snow, its chest rising and falling to the tempo of its dreams.

Or so she thinks. She hears a quiet nicker, looks up, and finds the mare sprawled across the stratosphere. It had watched, hypnotized, as she transformed into lotus, had timed its breaths to her own, and once her spirit leapt out of her body, its did the same. Loyalty and constancy cannot be constrained by the flesh; those are matters of the soul.

The two of them flow past and through each other. To the mare, who flips and spins and turns itself inside out, movement and freedom are no longer twins but one and the same. There is no barrier of skin, of species. The woman can ride on the mare, in it, as it. They immerse themselves in one another, tasting what it is to be horse, testing what it is to be human. They rest on the clouds. They coast on the clouds. A hawk passes through the mare, leaves a wing-shaped hole in its wake. At last, the mare can fly.

The setting sun drenches them both in gold. The light filters through them, and they refract it onto the world below, setting it ablaze. This also happens when they are in their bodies, though then the light is much harder to see. Bodies are dense and opaque. They shield but they shroud. Except for the eyes—that is where the light leaks out. The eyes' true purpose is not for seeing outside oneself. It is for seeing inside someone else.

The sun does not die; nothing does. It does not disappear, and from where the woman is now, she can see that it does not even set. That is merely the perspective one has while on the ground.

Night draws near, and she and the mare ride onward to meet it. The mare is a comet streaking through the skies, running rings around the planets, its tail streaming behind it. Horizons are no obstacle; it clears them with ease. The woman relishes the feeling of velocity, of infinity. After decades spent crawling, flight is such salvation. Nothing can stop her, not anymore.

And then, unexpectedly, something stops her: the sight of her husband, watching, waiting.

．　．　．

She does not believe what she is seeing. Have some pieces of cloud gotten caught in her eyes?

"I must be asleep," she says, turning her doubts into dreams, as she has trained herself to do. The mare has no uncertainty. It runs toward the husband and, in its excitement, runs inside him.

Man fills with mare. The homecoming is joyous. The sky shines with their cosmic embrace, with the constellation of the centaur.

Her husband stands before her, dazzling, incandescent. She cannot look at him for the brightness, yet she cannot look away. How could she have thought that a houseful of flames could destroy him? It is like thinking that a firefly could extinguish the sun.

He glows with anticipation. Again and again he has criss-crossed the dimensions to be by her side, has reached through the threshold to respond when she called. Finally, she has come to see where he lives.

The mare graciously slides out of him so that the woman can take its place, but surprise has shackled her, and she cannot move. For so long, his had been more a suggestion of a presence than an actual one. He was a man who lived inside her memories, a specter wandering her sleeping mind, the faintest trace of coriander and clove. Like a ventriloquist, he threw his voice and spoke to her through animals, rainstorms. Like a magician, he disappeared into thin air each time the curtains rose. Every encounter seemed a sleight of hand. What she is witnessing now, though, is no illusion. He is far more real—and far more alive—than she has ever seen him before.

"You're here," she says. It is both a question and an answer.

He laughs. "Where else could I be?"

His rays of warmth surround her; she feels she might combust. "This entire time, all I had to do to find you," she says, "was breathe in and out like a lotus and send myself into the stars?"

"Find me," he says. "I was lost?"

After so many years in the cold, the heat of him is nearly too much. It reignites every bitter winter, reminds her of a life spent frozen in ice.

"Along with everything else. You must have heard all my songs of loss. And they were not mine alone," she says. "Look at how much was taken from you."

"You cry that I have been silenced, that I never became father. I cannot even begin to tell you how much I am father now. You think it is a body that makes me a parent and a husband, that love is born from flesh and blood and not the other way around?"

"But why would you leave a world in which you can hold me?"

He is the full moon, bathing her, draping himself over her as she sleeps. The fog that greets her each morning and curls upon her shoulders. The steaminess of summer, inseparable from her own skin. "My little bird," he says, "I've never let you go."

She melts as he encircles her. Her memories start to thaw.

"Don't sing of loss. That's much too sad. Sing me a love song instead," he says, and when she touches his words, she finds they are made of light.

It has been a while since she has sung in that octave. A thread of sorrow unspools from her voice and winds around him. "I don't remember how it goes."

"I do," he says, and entwined with each other, illuminated with each other, they drift down to earth, through light-years and lifetimes, to listen to the opening notes of their song.

. . .

In the beginning, there is no he and no she. There is no life. There is nothing. The nothing is lonely with nothing around. It sings songs that are silent with nothingness. The sound is deafening. The songs grow so long and so plaintive that ultimately something notices them, for it is not enough for suffering to be voiced. It must also be heard.

Something resonates. The something reaches through the void, searching the darkness for its mother, unaware that the darkness is its mother. A cord forms between them.

The nothing, newly pregnant, expands. The child within quickens, making a sound that is deeper than oblivion, slower than stillness. In the chasm of the womb, the fire of labor starts. Fire is the home, the source of life, not its end.

The nothing screams as it contracts and rips apart. The act is excruciating, annihilating, one of violence as much as creation. All mothers have darkness; otherwise, they could not give birth to light. And it is from this pain that the everything is born. It is both something and all things, an only child and an every child, a soul and the soul.

The newborn soul opens its eyes, delighted to find itself incarnate. Its blood will turn to rivers, its limbs to redwoods. Its mouth will become beast, its heart human. Its eyes will be sea foam, its brows the crest of waves. As its chest rises and falls, so will empires. An in-breath will beget the woman, the out-breath her husband. They are what all lovers are: pieces of the same one sigh. They are themselves and yet they are each other and yet they are something greater than any of those, just as an inhalation and exhalation cannot be considered anything other than part of a single breath, and part of the breather. There is no distinction between them; there is no them. There is simply the soul. But that is the everything.

The soul has some growing to do first, before it is ready to be people. It is still figuring out who and what it is, as all children are. It needs a canvas on which to sketch itself, clay with which to craft itself, liquid mirrors in which to examine its face. And so it melts into mud, it hardens into rock, it sinks its toes in the dirt and feels what it is to be land. This is why, when joining together millennia later, lovers feel such connection. They are reliving the time when they were not yet distant hemispheres, remembering how they once fit perfectly together, re-creating their personal Pangaea in the arch of a foot curling around the knee, a head resting on a shoulder, fingers interlaced. This is why, when the fingers slide apart and the legs disentangle, the space between them may fill with oceans, may turn the lovers into islands. This is why separation can feel seismic.

The soul spends ages exploring the terrain of its body, progressing slowly, sedimentally. It is in no rush; mountains learn as much as men. But not all rocks enjoy sitting still. The fiery side of the soul takes to the skies as a meteor, then loses its footing and slips from space. Lightning strikes, literally. It sparks the land into life. The earth seethes. It is a primeval cauldron, the kind seen only in fairy tales and fevers. It boils over into a gooey soup of molecules that will one day build the pyramids.

The land differentiates. It carves itself into continents and then countries. Breaking itself into pieces while at the same time making itself more numerous: moving from one into many.

The molecules differentiate. A protozoon emerges, has some dreamy urge toward movement, and propels itself forward in a sudden spasm of evolution. Nitrogen and phosphorus develop a bond. Iron bleeds. Calcium clots. Oxygen is a breath of fresh air.

The organism differentiates. Mitosis is unleashed and uninhibited. Primordial cells transform into liver, horn, whisker. The soul curls into a snail, unfurls into a fern. A kingdom is established and dinosaurs wear the crown, but they are tyrants who use too much teeth. Mother Nature (Mother Nothing) sees the mischief that her child is getting into, grabs the dinosaurs by the scruff of their necks, and deposits them into the bodies of birds. Is this punishment? Is this death? No. Those heavy beings now soar. Faces and forelimbs are rearranged like puzzles, eggs hatch on the inside, bees learn to dance. Tiger gives birth to tabby, then their family becomes estranged. Humans look deep into the eyes of apes and call them animals.

Sound differentiates. Legs change to arms, knees and knuckles stand up straight, and in those first footsteps rhythm is born. Sex is song, a halting, haunting bass line of heartbeat and breath and bodies brushing against the grasses. A hunter spies a bird hidden in the branches, and to coax it out he imitates its mating call. The hunter finds more than a meal; he finds melody. His sister, pounding seeds into cake, finds drums. The bird is eaten, its bones cast aside. A starving child takes them. Her lips search the bone for meat; her eager breath fills its holes. Suddenly her hunger has a sound, a sharp one, which commands everyone around her to listen. Her flute differentiates too. It learns to sing not only of the hunger of the body but of the psyche, of sorrow and fear and other things that hollow the belly.

Language differentiates. It invents time and splits it into tenses. It sorts the world into singular and plural, as though these were antonyms. It circles the one soul, examining it from every angle, on an endless quest to discover its name. The ventured guesses pile atop one another, creating a thesaurus. *Hexagon. Starfish. Vermilion. God.*

The soul differentiates, now more than ever. It wants to know and to be all things, because that is to know and to be itself. By dividing, it multiplies: billions of bodies hosting one soul. It colors in the outline of the tiger and seeps through the stripes. It streaks through the naked notes of the bone flute, and it bobs and weaves behind the movements of a concerto. It remains a rock because it takes pleasure in permanence, and it turns into a human because it does not. It is the woman and her husband, and it becomes the woman and her husband.

The woman differentiates. So does her heart. She can see it now outside of her, in front of her—so giant, so drafty, and so inconceivably vast that it seems to belong not to her but to some enormous whale. Surely hers must be smaller, tighter, redder, meaner. She is amazed at its size. All this time she has lived in a mansion and never left the basement.

But there is too much focus on this, on the differentiating. As if there were any distinction between stone and cell and song, between man and molecule. As if they weren't a single soul in a single moment experiencing a single life in innumerable ways. As if the point of evolution were to branch off into many, rather than to find the way back to the one. As if union were not both the source and the destination, the first act and the final, the reason for division and the result.

As if the redwood weren't the woman experiencing a life of tree, and foam the life of sea. As if a mist of rain were not her soul suspended in water, and a sunrise her soul spreading throughout the sky. As if a nebulous fragment of her had not melted into the Milky Way; as if, when she looked into the stars at night, she were not looking at her reflection. As if the mare were an individual entity and not the part of her that had momentarily manifested as mare. As if the old man by the lake and the lake itself and every being immersed within it, every patient she ever played for, every wildflower and every wren, were not all she, and she were not all they. As if she were just herself, and not her own daughter, and not her own husband. As if separation were anything more than a sensation.

Touch one and you touch them all.

She had been wrong about songs of loss. There are no such things. It is not possible to lose someone when he is you. And it is not possible to lose yourself when you are everywhere. When the glassy-eyed blue jay and the blue jay flying across the fields and the cat that holds both between its teeth are each other, when they are the very same soul at the very same time, then what does death mean? Furthermore, what does life mean? Life as she knows it is happening only to the most minor portion of her.

She had been wrong about love songs too. They are not what you sing when you have found another person, but when you have found one of the million missing pieces of yourself.

. . .

Still, there is pleasure in splitting apart, because it allows for the pleasure of merging together. To move from one into more is a grand adventure. When you are one, you cannot find yourself. There is no need; you are already there. You live in the one room of your house. To become many is to crawl through the thickets of life and the oceans of death in search of who you are. It is to discover in everyone you meet the unseen faces of your soul, the unknown spaces of your heart.

Reunion is the only joy sweeter than union. And so the woman and the husband hide themselves in different bodies and seek themselves across the landscapes of time. They find each other in the deserts and as the deserts. They love each other as moss, as silt, as brushfire. As the dandelion and the wind that sends it dancing. To be human is not the end. They will evolve beyond that, in whatever form that takes. Or perhaps they will be formless altogether. She will be a thought and he a feeling. She will be a note of music, he another, and their daughter yet a third, and they will twine themselves around each other to create a chord, the basis of harmony.

She turns to him now. He reaches for her. He reaches inside her. He moves inside her. There is nothing to separate him from her anymore; the fire has burned all his boundaries away. He can be in her and never leave, outside her and around her all at once. And she has been calling this *loss?*

They caress each other's scars: where the flames singed his skin, where the oak tore her open. How do they touch without a body? They use all the bodies they have ever worn.

He is the mulberry moth, she the candle. He wraps his wings around her. Pulling away from her to become moth, coming closer to become light. Approaching her, withdrawing from her, engulfing her. Moth to light, moth away, moth to light, away. Fluttering, flickering. He clings to her light, she clings to his wings. She lights him on fire. Now moth is light.

She is the curtain, he the breeze that blows her back and forth. He is a sea of air, a wave of wind on which she sails. He pushes her away, he calls her near. Teasing her, lifting her to him, wafting through her. In and out, in and out. She floats, weightless, on the rhythm of his tide.

He is the hummingbird, bringing beak to honeysuckle. Drawing closer, drinking her in, consuming her. Flying away, flying back, drunk on her. His entire life the flower.

She is the river, he the stones of the bed over which she flows, every current a kiss.

He is the lightning cleaving the sky, she the thunder roaring in the wake of his fire. His sizzle and her shout.

The moon swimming in shadow, hungry for heat. The sun behind it, enveloping it, igniting it. Moon dissolving into sun, into a brilliance that blinds all who dare look.

The bow pressing itself against the violin, stroking her neck until she cries out with song.

The stained-glass dragonfly worshipping at the altar of the lotus, rapturous with prayer.

The trembling aspen, shaking from the slightest touch.

The glacier advancing, receding, touching ice, melting ice.

The weft, utterly powerless not to coil itself around the warp.

The husband and the woman, sighing and desiring each other into and out of existence.

The soul coming together, breaking apart. Reflecting itself, resurrecting itself. Electrifying the body, surpassing the body. Differentiating and combining. Cleaving and clinging. Dividing and multiplying. Separating and uniting.

Separating.

And uniting.

Over and over.

Without time.

Without end.

That is the everything.

~

Coda

A body can contain only so many days and the woman's not
many more, so when her husband says, "Stay with me,"
she is tempted to surrender the rest. The old are often granted
this privilege, to glide out of a life and into a sleep so comfortable that return is neither necessary nor desired. And why
would she choose to carve herself into pieces again, to submit
to separation when union is all she has ever sought?

"Stay with me," he says. "Isn't that what you want?"

It is precisely what she wants. But she cannot leave her love
song in the skies, unwritten, unheard. The final music lesson
is not for her to receive but to impart. She must teach the soul
what it was to be woman, what it was to be her. She must tell it
everything she has come to know so that it can come to know

itself. And there is only one language in which she is eloquent enough to describe such things.

Her decision surprises her even as she speaks it aloud. "I have to go back."

And so one more time, one millionth time, they pull apart. She shivers as his spirit slips out of her and emptiness takes his place. However, this is nothing to mourn. Again and again, in a bed that glowed with moonlight, he had done the same with his body, yet she had never mistaken the parting as permanent.

She beckons for the mare to come. *Are you ready for one last ride?*

The mare knows that it is no longer needed, that it has given her all the music it possesses. The meter of its hooves clip-clopping through the seasons. The vibrato of its whinny, the staccato twitch of its tail, the ostinato of its fidelity. Its bones are nearly as old as hers, and it too can choose whether to relinquish them or rekindle them. It does not need to ask her permission, but it asks, because no one ever has.

"Go," she tells it, and there is no grief, not this high up.

With her word, the mare erupts with light, or what some call death. Before her eyes it becomes a foal once more. It has stayed by her side throughout her entire journey. Now its own is about to begin.

"Good-bye, friend," the woman murmurs, though the mare is already long gone, running wild through the night.

. . .

The woman's body is lying where she left it. A few lotus breaths bring her back inside. It takes her a moment to regain her bearings, as can happen when one comes down from the clouds. Her eyes and hands search the surroundings. There is her harp. There is her book. There is her mare, cold and rigid. She looks around her, at the bare tree branches shaking with laughter in the wind, at the moon slinking across the sky, casting silver shadows on the ice. No. *There* is her mare.

She covers its body with snow, with a kiss.

She enters the cabin, sits at the desk, and places *Music Lessons* in front of her. This is her story; this is her score. She could rewrite it, rip out the pages, insist upon waltzes and not requiems, and neither her life nor her notation would ever know sadness. To play the music in a major or a minor key: this is the choice of the composer, not the composition.

She turns to the blank pages and begins to fill them with sound.

She draws the staff by hand, that loom through which she threads her notes and weaves her tune.

The treble clef is a curling plume of smoke.

Can music exist without time? Why not? Life does. In place of a time signature, she puts only a dot.

Is life an étude, an exercise, a place to hone one's skills? An improvisation or an opus? She writes: To be played GRAVE, SERIOUS. But something that is meant to be played should not be so serious. She revises it: To be played FORTISSIMO, VERY

STRONG—with all the power of a butterfly. This is not quite right, either. She crosses out both instructions and decides: AD LIBITUM, AT THE DISCRETION OF THE PERFORMER.

Four notes are all that are needed to compose the human, the falcon, the masterpiece. This, too, shall be her scale.

The passages climb the heavens and plummet into pitch-black caves. The chords are inversions, because everything is an inversion. A child dying inside, instead of living outside. A man turning to dust. Loss turning to learning.

PLAY THESE PASSAGES AGAIN. AND AGAIN. AND AGAIN. She'd made her sorrow a leitmotif. This is not music; it is madness. She pauses for a moment and writes: THEN, PLAY THEM NO MORE.

Her life had been so full of the accidental, always deviating from the expected. Everything seemed a mistake. Now that she is lucid, nothing could be less so. She adds the accidentals to her piece. Grief flattens the spirit. Pain sharpens the heart. She changes them to naturals. The notes decay, just like bodies. She allows this, knowing that they will be born again in the next measure.

She sings the lyrics aloud. LITTLE BIRD, BLUE BIRD, WHY OH WHY SO BLUE? BECAUSE IT ATE A BLUE FRUIT. *And forgot to taste its sweetness,* the woman chides herself. *Little bird, don't you know that is what the fruit is for?*

She transposes the little bird into a swan, mute until the moment of its death, when it finally bursts with all the beauty it could not speak in life. Whose song is not a lament but a hallelujah.

For the mare, she composes movement after movement.

She had asked the king and queen to resurrect her husband, yet she is the one who brings him back. He reappears in each piece she writes. He comes alive in each phrase. Fire did not steal his breath, for he breathes life into her and inspires every note. She had not realized that all along it was they who could turn themselves immortal, and that death is as powerless against art as it is against love.

She compresses her years into measures, arranges her memories into harmonies. The fermata of being lost in the forest. The faint ghost notes, sensed more than heard. The tempo rubato of the waters of time. An act of compassion, enclosed in repeat signs. HOLD THIS NOTE. HOLD IT FOREVER. The baritone beats of her old, whalelike heart; the snaky cadence of venom entering its chambers. The furious conducting of the antlike being, without whom the music would have ended too soon—or never begun. The glissando of sliding along the cord between the mother and the stars. The melody of the sparrow, who taught the warrior in her how to turn suffering into song. The ascending arpeggio of love, which keeps rising higher and higher and—oh! It's just flown off the ledger lines. The eternal trill between angel and human, human and angel.

Last, the conclusion. The rest. THE END.

As if such a thing were even possible! DA CAPO AL CODA, she writes. PLAY FROM THE BEGINNING.

Once she was anonymous. Now she has learned who she is, and on the last page of the book she signs her names with a flourish:

ARIA.

THE OAK.

THE HIGHER SELF.

THE EVERYTHING.

She picks up the harp. The white light forms from her hands. It spreads along the staffs and sets the songs on fire. The strings, as she touches them, become silky and loose. One by one, they pull away from the soundboard, mulberry moths circling a willow that weeps no more. Still she plays on. She does not need the instrument. She is the instrument.

The light swells inside her, presses against her, too bright for her body to constrain any longer. Softly, lovingly, it cracks her shell open and releases her. Movement. Freedom. She takes to the skies. There is no difference anymore between sound and silence, music and moth and man. These are simply the scattered pieces of her making their way back to the one.

The warm sea of the night sky envelops them all.

It enfolds them in its arms.

It whispers, "Welcome home."

⸘

Reprise

"*H*ere you are, my little bird."

The woman opens her eyes.

She is lying beside the lake of time, warming herself on its banks, drying the decades from her wings.

"And here you are," she says. It is not a question anymore. It is as clear as the water that stretches before her. Why had she insisted on turning reality into such a riddle?

Her husband smiles. "Where else could I be?"

From far off, she can hear the voice of the old man instructing some lost soul to go deeper.

The splash of a diver slicing through the depths of time.

The laughter of her daughter playing around in water and in bodies.

The thunder of hoofbeats galloping across the sky. The mare finally catching the sun.

Centuries float past the woman and her husband. Yesterdays drift in the breeze. Forever quietly laps against the shores where they sit and watch the generations come and go.

His words are a ripple across the lake, an echo in her ear: "What would you like to do now?"

It is what he asks in her dreams. Is she dreaming?

No. She is awake.

She says, "I'd like to grow."

"How shall we love each other next?" he asks. "As mangroves, canyons, companions? Let us be twin brothers or twin flames. Or you could be an oyster, and I the pearl you cradle and make glow."

"As all of those," she tells him, for they are but different names to call oneself, different mirrors of the same face. "As everything."

"I will be a doctor and bring you to life with my touch."

"I will do the same," she says.

"We could live among war."

"We'd learn much that way."

"Or among roses and buttercups."

"That way, too."

Somewhere in the world, two spirits are twining themselves around each other, calling to her, composing the chords of her body and the pulse of her heart. The sound draws her to the water's edge.

What was it like to be human? It is like trying to recall the details of a dream she'd had as a child. In the distance four notes begin to play, faintly at first, and then rolling like a mist along the lake. Something ancient and familiar reverberates within her, a melody forgotten by the mind yet remembered by the bones.

Her husband stands next to her, enticed by the strains of his own theme.

Time calls her closer, invites her inside.

Once she had asked herself why she would have entered it at all.

This is her answer. It was for the music, for the beautiful music.

For the chance to become, for one brief and thrilling moment, a song.

Their daughter waves to them from the center of the lake. *Come on in. The water's fine.*

Her husband reaches for her. "Shall we dive together?"

He is my teacher and *he is my neighbor* and *he is my sister* and *he is my husband* and *he is my wife* and *he is my child* and *he is my self.*

"We always do," she replies.

They take another step forward.

He turns to her for one last look at her light. "Come find me," he says, "and sing me a love song."

As if there could be any other kind. The woman laughs.

Then she leaps and lets go.

Acknowledgments

Thank you to everyone at Hay House for welcoming me so warmly into your family. I deeply appreciate everyone who worked on this book. Thank you to Sally Mason-Swaab, Stacy Horowitz, and Mollie Langer. Patty Gift, you are a wonderful editor, friend, and teacher. You show me what it is to be gentle, patient, and gracious; you shaped this book, and me along with it. Reid Tracy, thank you for your vision and your trust and for taking a chance on this book. My world has turned on your kindness.

Massimiliano Ungaro, if only all writers could have a first reader as special as you, one who reads with his heart. Thank you for helping me grow. Thank you to Rachel Sullivan for your thoughtful edits, to Kimberly Clark Sharp for your wisdom, and to Dave Bricker for your artistry.

My family and friends were a great source of support during the writing process, in particular Jordan Weiss, Darrah Gilderman, Jennifer Williams, Jill Cohen, Lydia Grunstra, and Vanessa Benitez.

Schnitzel, you were by my side for every single word, tirelessly teaching me of loyalty and love.

Finally, thank you to my incredible mother and father, without whom this book would not exist. Your generosity, encouragement, and support are as limitless as the universe. I am forever grateful to you. You have given me 40,000 years of love—and so much more.

Reader's Guide

1. The book opens with the concept of souls planning their lives before birth, as the husband and the woman select certain experiences and people to be part of their lives. Do you believe that such planning takes place prior to incarnation?

2. Think about the important people in your life. Could your souls have met and made certain agreements before your lives began? What might these people be here to teach you? Why might you have wanted them to be a part of your life? Does your answer change depending on whether a person has had a positive or negative impact on you? If you chose to interact with these people in order to learn and to grow, is there such a thing as a "negative" impact?

3. Although the woman plans her life before it begins, she states these plans can be altered. What are your thoughts about free will? How does it interact with destiny? Do they both

exist? Can they both exist at the same time? Is one more dominant than the other, and if so, which one?

4. A powerful connection exists between humans and animals, both wild and domesticated. The mare is intuitively aware of the woman's feelings and thoughts. Do you feel that the animals and/or pets in your life share this same ability? What have they taught you? What have they shown you about yourself that you otherwise might not have known? In what ways might an animal's consciousness be more limited than that of humans, and in what ways might it be more expansive?

5. Have you ever sensed the presence of someone who has died? How did this make you feel? Do you believe that people who have died can still be around you? How close do you think they are?

6. The old man tells the woman that "the earth turns on a kindness." Was there a time in your life when someone showed a kindness to you, whether small or large, that touched you deeply? How did this kindness transform your day, your thoughts, or your emotions?

7. What do you think about the idea of parallel universes? Do they exist? Do we come into contact with them? What might your life be like in a parallel universe?

8. In your opinion, what happens after you die?

9. Do you believe that you create your own reality? To what degree is your reality created by your thoughts, beliefs, desires, and emotions? How is your outer reality a reflection of your inner reality? When has changing one changed the other?

10. The woman learns that the most important moment of her life was a kindness that she doesn't even remember performing. What if life were measured in kindnesses rather than wealth, titles, and achievements? How would your definition of a successful life change? Would you consider yourself successful under this definition? What could you do to be more successful?

11. Think of an occasion when you showed a person, animal, or plant unconditional love, if only briefly. Imagine how it must have felt for the other to receive your love. How did this help the soul of that person, animal, or plant? How did it help your own soul?

12. If your life were a song, what kind of song would it be (a pop song, the blues, a classical symphony, etc.)? What would it sound like? Could you make it a different kind of song, if you wanted? What would you change it to? What would the lyrics be? Who is composing your song?

About the Author

Amy Weiss has a BA from Columbia University, an MFA in Fiction Writing from Washington University in St. Louis, and an MSW from Barry University. She is a licensed clinical social worker and the co-author of *Miracles Happen*. *Crescendo* is her first novel. Find out more at: www.Amy-Weiss.com

We hope you enjoyed this Hay House Visions book. If you'd like to receive our online catalog featuring additional information on Hay House books and products, or if you'd like to find out more about the Hay Foundation, please contact:

VISIONS

Hay House, Inc., P.O. Box 5100, Carlsbad, CA 92018-5100
(760) 431-7695 or (800) 654-5126
(760) 431-6948 (fax) or (800) 650-5115 (fax)
www.hayhouse.com® • www.hayfoundation.org

• • •

Published and distributed in Australia by: Hay House Australia Pty.
Ltd., 18/36 Ralph St., Alexandria NSW 2015 • *Phone:* 612-9669-4299 *Fax:* 612-9669-4144 • www.hayhouse.com.au

Published and distributed in the United Kingdom by: Hay House UK, Ltd.,
Astley House, 33 Notting Hill Gate, London W11 3JQ • *Phone:* 44-20-3675-2450 *Fax:* 44-20-3675-2451 • www.hayhouse.co.uk

Published and distributed in the Republic of South Africa by: Hay House SA (Pty), Ltd.,
P.O. Box 990, Witkoppen 2068 info@hayhouse.co.za • www.hayhouse.co.za

Published in India by: Hay House Publishers India, Muskaan Complex,
Plot No. 3, B-2, Vasant Kunj, New Delhi 110 070 • *Phone:* 91-11-4176-1620 • *Fax:* 91-11-4176-1630 • www.hayhouse.co.in

Distributed in Canada by: Raincoast Books, 2440 Viking
Way, Richmond, B.C. V6V 1N2 • *Phone:* 1-800-663-5714 • *Fax:* 1-800-565-3770 • www.raincoast.com

• • •

Take Your Soul on a Vacation

Visit www.HealYourLife.com® to regroup, recharge, and reconnect with your own magnificence. Featuring blogs, mind-body-spirit news, and life-changing wisdom from Louise Hay and friends.

Visit www.HealYourLife.com today!

Free e-newsletters
from Hay House, the Ultimate
Resource for Inspiration

Be the first to know about Hay House's dollar deals, free downloads, special offers, affirmation cards, giveaways, contests, and more!

 Get exclusive excerpts from our latest releases and videos from *Hay House Present Moments*.

 Enjoy uplifting personal stories, how-to articles, and healing advice, along with videos and empowering quotes, within *Heal Your Life*.

 Have an inspirational story to tell and a passion for writing? Sharpen your writing skills with insider tips from *Your Writing Life*.

Sign Up Now!

Get inspired, educate yourself, get a complimentary gift, and share the wisdom!

http://www.hayhouse.com/newsletters.php

Visit www.hayhouse.com to sign up today!

 HAY HOUSE

HAYHOUSE RADIO
radio for your soul

HealYourLife.com